THE *SHADOWERS*

DONALD HAMILTON

A **MATT HELM**

THE *NOVEL*

SHADOWERS

TITAN BOOKS

The Shadowers
Print edition ISBN: 9780857683373
E-book edition ISBN: 9781781162361

Published by Titan Books
A division of Titan Publishing Group Ltd
144 Southwark Street, London SE1 0UP

First edition: December 2013
1 2 3 4 5 6 7 8 9 10

Did you enjoy this book? We love to hear from our readers.
Please email us at readerfeedback@titanemail.com or write to us at
Reader Feedback at the above address.

To receive advance information, news, competitions, and exclusive
offers online, please sign up for the Titan newsletter on our website:
www.titanbooks.com

THE *SHADOWERS*

1

When I came hurriedly out of the hotel, the car was waiting for me. It was white with letters in gold: REDONDO BEACH—CITY POLICE. They seem to be painting all police cars white these days. I guess it makes them easier to keep clean. The uniformed man at the wheel threw the door open and leaned over.

"Mr. Corcoran?"

"I'm Corcoran," I said.

Well, I was, as far as Redondo Beach, Florida, was concerned. The fact that I might have other names else-where—in Washington, D.C., for instance—was nobody's business down here where I was spending a month's well-earned rest in the sun. At least I hoped it wasn't.

"Please get in, sir," the policeman said.

I got in and he had us going before the door had closed. He switched on his flasher and cut around the block sharply.

"Where did it happen?" I asked.

"South along the Miami highway a few miles. At least that's where they told me to take you."

"Is she badly hurt?"

He didn't look at me. "You talked with Headquarters, sir; you know more than I do. All I know is I'm supposed to get you there fast."

He hit a button and the siren cut short the conversation. For a city cop in a city cop car he had highway patrol ideas. We shot through the late evening traffic like a runaway missile. Near the edge of town we picked up another red flasher ahead. That was the ambulance heading for the scene. My man cut around it and slowed a bit to stay with it, breaking trail.

It was a good try on everybody's part, but when we got there I saw at once it hadn't been quite good enough. There were two state cars and some other cars and a number of people; and those people had stopped caring when we'd arrive because they knew there was no longer anything for us to do. That race had been won by the gent on the pale horse. They were more interested, now, in watching the Cadillac burn.

We circled to get over to the northbound side of the highway, and parked behind the other official cars. A state policeman came up as I got out.

"Mr. Corcoran?" he said. "I'm sorry."

"Where is she?" I asked.

"Down this way," he said. "She was thrown clear. If they won't wear seat belts—"

I said, "I know. It's much better to stay with the car.

Particularly when it's an open convertible that first rolls and then burns like a torch."

He glanced around, started to get annoyed, and thought better of it. We'd reached our destination, anyway. There was a uniformed man standing by the blanket-covered form on the ground.

The man who'd brought me said, "I'd better warn you... Well, she must have been doing damn close to ninety when she missed the curve."

I bent down and pulled the blanket back and had my look, then replaced the cover and walked off a little ways until I stood looking down at something gleaming in the rank grass. It was a silver evening pump to go with the dress she'd worn. I reflected on women's shoes and how they never could seem to stay on in a crisis. If the final cataclysm overtakes the human race, I decided, the last trace of womankind left behind in the smoldering wreckage will be a scorched, radioactive slipper with a high, slim heel.

It was better to formulate this deep philosophy than to remember that we'd quarreled. Take a womp with money and a man without and the dialogue at a certain point in the relationship hardly needs repeating, particularly if both parties are fairly bullheaded. It had started with a party she'd wanted us to go to at the big house of some wealthy acquaintances of hers who didn't think any more of me than I did of them. It had ended with her driving to the party alone. And driving back alone, still angry, unhappy, and probably a little tight...

"Mr. Corcoran?" It was the state cop who believed in sticking loyally with your car even if it squashed and incinerated you. "I'm sorry to bother you, sir, but we need a little information. Could you give me your wife's full name for the report?"

I said, "She wasn't my wife."

He said quickly, "But we distinctly understood—"

"So I gathered," I said. "When the police called me at the hotel, they asked first if my wife drove a white Cadillac convertible with Texas plates. Since I was more interested in learning why they were calling than in keeping my matrimonial record straight, I said yes. The lady's name was Mrs. Gail Hendricks. She was divorced from Mr. Hendricks, whoever he may be. I never met him. She came from Midland, Texas. There are some relatives there, I believe. What made you think she was my wife?"

"She was wearing a wedding ring. She asked for you."

"You could get into trouble, making deductions like that," I said.

"What is your full name, Mr. Corcoran?"

"Paul," I said. "Paul William Corcoran. Newspaperman. From Denver, Colorado."

Well, that's what it said on the cards in my wallet. My real name is Matthew Helm, but it figures in too many official dossiers for me to wear it carelessly, even on leave. And while I'm technically a government employee, certain people in Washington prefer that my exact duties remain unspecified, as far as the general public is concerned.

"And what was your relationship to Mrs. Hendricks?" the policeman asked.

"We'd known each other for a couple of years," I said. "We were staying at the same hotel by prearrangement. The Redondo Towers. If that's a relationship, you name it."

He hesitated, a little embarrassed by my candor. "I'll say the identification was made by a friend of the deceased," he said, and that's the way it went down in the record.

There was no reason to think the accident was anything but what it seemed, except that accidents are always suspect in my line of business. I hung around long enough, therefore, to make the routine checks, trying not to show any more interest, however, than would be expected from a friend of the deceased who was also a reporter. When they could move in on the car, they found no indication that it had been gimmicked in any way. The body, said the doctor, displayed no signs of violence. I couldn't help wondering just what he called being hurled from a car at ninety miles per hour—I mean, how violent can you get?—but his general drift was clear.

When I got back to my hotel room at last, I took the little knife from my pocket. You could call it a large pocket knife or a small folding hunting knife. It was more or less a duplicate of one I had broken in the line of duty. I'd happened to complain about the loss, and Gail had secretly given the description to a well-known and expensive knife-maker and surprised me with the handsome result.

She'd been trying to give me things ever since we came down here together. It isn't smart to accept presents from people—particularly women—who have more money than you have, but I hadn't been able to turn down this particular gift without seeming stuffy and unappreciative. I mean, a wealthy woman can give a man a watch or even a car without signifying much more than that she's got money to throw away; but when a woman gives a man in my line of work a weapon, knowing how it's apt to be used, it means something special. It means she has faced and accepted certain things about him. That was before we'd quarreled, of course.

I shoved the knife back in my pocket, went downstairs, and called Washington from a pay phone in the lobby. There was nothing I could do here that would make any difference now, and I don't like hanging around to bury people. I said I was tired of being lazy and asked if they could use me. The answer was yes.

Two hours later I was flying kitty-corner across the Gulf of Mexico on my way to New Orleans, Louisiana.

2

I'd been told to maintain my cover as Paul Corcoran, Denver newspaperman, for the time being, and to register at the Montclair Hotel in New Orleans under this name. Since I'd requested immediate work, I was being shoved late into a going operation, and there wasn't time to build me a new identity.

After getting a room at the hotel, I made contact according to instructions, never mind with whom. I wouldn't know him if I saw him on the street, myself. He was just a voice on the phone. He told me—it was morning by this time—to spend the day sight-seeing, which is a technical term for making damn sure you're not being watched.

Reporting back in the evening with the all-clear signal, I was told to leave the hotel casually, on foot, a certain exact number of minutes before midnight. I was to walk in a certain direction at a certain pace. If a red Austin-Healey sports job pulled up beside me, and the driver wore a Navy uniform and uttered a certain phrase, I was to answer him with another phrase and get into the car.

The upshot of these Hollywood maneuvers was that just before dawn I found myself on a motor launch crossing Pensacola Bay, which put me back in Florida again after a wild night drive, but near the top of the state instead of the bottom. There was an aircraft carrier anchored out in the bay. It loomed over the still water massive and motionless, as if set on permanent concrete foundations. It was as easy to imagine the Pentagon putting out to sea.

I glanced at the lights of the Naval Air Station from which we'd come, bid terra firma a silent farewell, and scrambled onto the platform at the foot of the long, flimsy stairway suspended from ropes—a ladder, in Navy terminology—that ran slantingly up the ship's side to a lighted opening far above. My escort was beside me, ready to keep me from falling in the drink.

He was a trim young fellow with a shiny gold stripe-and-a-half on each shoulder of his immaculate khaki gabardine uniform, and a shiny Naval Academy ring on his left hand. There were shiny gold wings on his chest, and a neat little plastic name plate, white on black, reading J.S. BRAITHWAITE. He waved the launch away. This left us stranded on the rickety platform just a few feet above the water, with no place to go but up.

"After you, sir," he said. "Remember, you salute the quarterdeck first, then the O.O.D."

"Quarterdeck," I said. "I thought quarterdecks went

out with sail." I glanced at the two-and-a-half stripes on the shoulder of the uniform I had been supplied for the occasion. The change of costume had been made in an empty apartment in town.

"You're a lieutenant commander, sir," he said. "The quarterdeck is aft, that way." He pointed.

I started climbing, trying to fight off the sense of unreality that came of switching location and identity too fast. I saluted the quarterdeck and the O.O.D., as Braithwaite had called him—the Officer of the Deck— who wore a pair of binoculars hung around his neck and looked sleepy and bored. I guess the early-morning watch is a bitch in any service, uniformed or otherwise. I followed my guide along a vast empty hangar space to a stairway—excuse me, ladder—leading down. Presently, after negotiating a maze of narrow passages below, I found myself in a white-painted cabin with a single bunk.

"You can flake out there if you like, sir," Braithwaite said. "They're still in conference. They won't be needing you for a while. Would you like some coffee?"

In the business, we go on the assumption that, among friends at least, we'll be told what we need to know when the time comes for us to know it. I didn't ask who was in conference, therefore, but I did drink the coffee. Then, left alone, I shed my uniform blouse, stretched out on the bunk, closed my eyes, and tried not to think of a shape under a blanket and a single silver slipper. After a while I went to sleep.

When I awoke, my watch read well past eight, but the

cabin had no direct connection with the outside world, so I had to take daylight on faith. I noticed a certain vibration and deduced that we were under way. Presently Braithwaite appeared and guided me down the passage to the plumbing, after which he took me to the wardroom for breakfast.

I knew it was the wardroom because it said so on the door. We had a table to ourselves, but there were other officers present who looked me over casually as I sat down. I hoped I didn't look as phony as I felt in my borrowed uniform.

"We don't want to make a mystery of you, sir," Braithwaite said. "As far as the ship's company is concerned, you're just a reserve officer on temporary active duty observing carrier training operations for the day. There'll be less talk that way than if we tried to hide you from sight." He glanced at his watch. "We should have some advanced jet trainers coming in shortly. As soon as we've finished chow, we'll go topside and watch them practice landings to make it look good. I hope you don't mind a little noise."

He grinned. I didn't get the significance of the grin just then, but it became clear to me a little later, as I stood on a narrow observation walk on the carrier's superstructure, or island, looking down at the flight deck, which was the length of three football fields, with catapults forward and arresting gear aft, all explained to me in detail by my conscientious young escort. We were well out in the Gulf of Mexico by this time, out of sight of land on a clear, bright, cool fall day, and the ship was steaming into the wind fast enough that I had to pull my uniform cap down hard to keep it from being blown away. Braithwaite laughed.

"We've got to have thirty-two knots of wind along the flight deck to take the jets aboard," he said. "This time of year there's usually a breeze to help out, but in summer, in a flat calm, the engineering officer has to sweat blood to make it. Here they come now, sir."

They were already circling the ship like a swarm of hornets; now the first one came in fast, snagged an arresting wire with its tailhook, and slammed to a stop. It was hardly clear and taxiing forward, past the island where we stood, when the second one hit the wires—and I began to understand Braithwaite's remark about noise. The damn planes roared, shrieked, sobbed, and whistled. The port catapult would fling one thundering jet off the bow to go around again, while another blasted away on the starboard catapult, awaiting its turn. Meanwhile number three was taxiing up amidships, howling up a storm, and number four was coming in over the stem, screaming like a banshee...

There was something hypnotic about the tremendous din. It brought back memories of other places I'd stood some years ago watching other planes take off, planes that upon occasion I'd helped prepare the way for in secret and unpleasant ways. I don't suppose the kids in those planes ever knew that anybody had been before them, any more than these earnest kids with their faces half hidden by their helmets and mikes realized that if the time ever came for them to take their deadly machines up armed, they would be contributing only a little official noise and glamor to the silent, unofficial war that's always being fought by quiet people without flashy helmets and often without microphones, too, or any other means of communicating with home base. What we undercover services needed, I thought wryly, was a public relations department. People just didn't appreciate us.

Suddenly the planes were gone, and it was quiet again except for the wind and the muted rumbling of the ship's machinery. Braithwaite glanced at his watch.

"Just about time for the HUP to pick up the brass from Washington," he said. "There she is, right off the quarter."

A clattering sound broke the relative peace, and a banana-shaped helicopter with two rotors settled to the deck right below us. Three men—two dignified civilians and an Army officer with a lot of fancy stuff on his cap—made their way out to the chopper, climbed aboard, and were borne away to the north. I glanced at Braithwaite. He showed me a smooth young poker face, so I didn't deem it advisable to start a discussion of the fact that we'd just seen three fairly important people whose faces would be recognized by almost every alert newspaper reader or TV viewer. On the other, hand it didn't seem likely I'd been shown them by accident. Somebody was trying to impress me with the importance of the forthcoming job, whatever it might be. Braithwaite made reference to his watch again; the boy was a real chronometer fiend.

"Well, they should be just about ready for you below, sir," he said, and showed me to the door, or hatch, by which we'd come out. "Watch your head going down the ladder…"

I couldn't tell you exactly where aboard the ship the little movie theater was, but it had obviously just seen use as a conference room, judging by the scattered paper, empty glasses, full ashtrays, and the smell of tired tobacco smoke. There were only two people in it now. One was a woman. The first impression she made on me can best be described by saying that after a brief glance to make sure I didn't recognize her, I looked at the man.

He was lean and gray-haired, with black eyebrows. He wore a charcoal-gray flannel suit, a neat white shirt, a conservative silk tie, and he may have looked like a well-preserved middle-aged banker or businessman to some people, but he'd never look like that to me. I happened to know he was one of the half-dozen most dangerous and ruthless men in the world.

I recognized him, all right. I should, having worked for him for well over fifteen years, off and on.

Mac said, "Thank you, Mr. Braithwaite. Wait next door, if you please."

"Yes, sir."

Mac watched the young lieutenant (jg) turn smartly and depart. He smiled briefly. "They train them well up there on the Severn, don't they?"

I wasn't particularly interested in Braithwaite's training, but if Mac wanted to apply the casual touch I'd play along, for a while at least.

"He's a good boy," I said. "He hasn't allowed himself to be human once, so far. And he drives a sports car like an artist. But he's going to sir me to death if he isn't careful."

Mac said, "I seem to recall another young officer who had a predilection for that word. He was a pretty good driver, too."

"Yes, sir," I said. "But, sir, I don't think you'll have as much luck getting this one to switch services, sir. He likes the Navy, sir."

Mac shrugged. "I'll make a note of his name nevertheless. There may come a time, world conditions being what they are, when personal preferences will again have to be disregarded. Not that you were hard to persuade, if I remember correctly."

I said, "I always was a bloodthirsty kid. I don't think this one's quite mean enough for you."

"Well, we'll see." He studied me appraisingly. "You look fit. The rest has done you good."

"Yes, sir."

"I was sorry to hear about the lady's accident."

I looked at him for a moment. He'd never approved of my interest in Gail Hendricks. He'd thought her a spoiled bitch, rich and unreliable, not at all the sort of dedicated, dutiful little girl he preferred to have his men associate with, if they couldn't be satisfied with professional entertainment. We have, of course, no real private life. All our attachments, amorous and otherwise, are a matter of record in the Washington office.

I said, "I'm sure you cried all the way to the filing cabinet to pull her card, sir."

He didn't call me down for disrespect. He just said, "Of course you took steps to determine that it *was* an accident."

"Yes, sir. She was upset, for personal reasons we don't have to go into here. She'd had too much to drink. She was driving much too fast. It was a long, sweeping curve and she swung out toward the edge a little too far and tried to come back. They think all they need are power brakes and power steering to make two tons of luxury machinery handle like a stripped-down racing Ferrari. At that speed, she'd be riding the damn curve right at the limit of tire adhesion for a car that big. When she hauled on the wheel, the Cad started to slide. She panicked and hit the brakes and everything broke loose and she went off into the trees. There was no evidence of sabotage or any other fancy monkey business. There were no bullet wounds, hypo marks, or unexplained bruises. Somebody could simply have pulled alongside and forced her over, of course, but there's no indication that anybody did."

Mac grimaced. "I don't like accidents involving our people. There's always a question. Well, I'll keep in touch in case they should turn up something, but we can't spend any more time on it now."

He glanced at the woman standing nearby, waiting. When he looked her way, she came forward to join us. At close range, I saw that I'd done her a slight injustice in dismissing her with a glance. It was the makeup, or lack of it, that had fooled me. There was also the straight, mousy, pulled-back hair and the horn-rimmed glasses.

She was moderately tall. Her bulky tweed suit made her figure hard to judge correctly. The straight, loose-fitting jackets currently fashionable may come in handy to disguise an unwanted pregnancy—a problem this lady wasn't likely to have to face, I judged—but they can hardly be called flattering. Her sensible shoes did nothing for her legs and ankles. Still, she wasn't obese, emaciated, or deformed.

As for her face, it had a lot of forehead and chin, as well as a grim, unhappy mouth. I put her age between thirty and thirty-five, although it could have been less. I decided that I didn't like her. There's really no excuse for a potentially presentable female to deliberately go around looking like Lady Macbeth after a hard night with the knife. I mean, it's a kind of reverse vanity that implies a lot of real conceit somewhere.

While I was looking her over, she was giving me a thorough examination from hair to toenails. She turned to Mac and spoke without enthusiasm.

"This is your alternate candidate, Mr. McRae? Isn't he rather tall for an agent? I supposed they were all fairly inconspicuous people."

"This is Mr. Paul Corcoran," Mac said, passing over the personal comments. "Paul, Dr. Olivia Mariassy."

Dr. Olivia Mariassy barely acknowledged the introduction with a nod my way. "I suppose that's an alias," she said to Mac. "It's a poor choice. The man is obviously of Scandinavian descent, not Irish." Still speaking to Mac, she frowned at me: "Well, at least he doesn't have the slick, ivy-league look of the other prospect. I don't think I could stomach that crew cut and that button-down collar very long, not to mention the pipe. I think a pipe is nearly always an affectation, don't you? Do you smoke?"

The final question was thrown at me. "No, ma'am," I said. "Not unless my cover requires it."

"Cover?"

"Disguise."

"I see. Well, that's something," she said. "Only a fool would poison himself with coal tar and nicotine after all the evidence that has been published. Do you drink?"

"Yes, ma'am," I said. "I also run around with women. But I don't gamble. Honest."

That got me another long look through the horn-rimmed glasses. "Well," she said, "a rudimentary sense of humor is better than none at all, I suppose."

Mac said, "Mr. Corcoran's training and experience—"

"Please! I'm not questioning the professional qualifications of either candidate. I'm sure they are both very rapid on the draw, if that's the proper phrase. I'm sure they're both capable and ruthless and perfectly horrible. Do you play chess?"

She'd aimed that one at me. "A little," I said.

Olivia Mariassy frowned thoughtfully. There was a brief silence. Her head came up. "Well, he'll have to do. The other was quite impossible. If I have to marry one of them, I'll take this one." She turned away and bent over a worn briefcase on one of the theater seats, took out a small black book and handed it to me. It was Capablanca's *Chess Fundamentals*. "You'd better study that, Mr. Corcoran," she said. "It will give us something to do on our honeymoon. Good-bye, Mr. McRae. I'll leave the arrangements to you. Just let me know what you want me to do."

We watched her walk out with her briefcase. Mac didn't speak and neither did I. I won't say I couldn't. I just didn't try.

3

Down inside the big ship where we were—wherever that was—there wasn't a thing to be heard except the steady, everpresent rumble of the heavy propulsion machinery. All the planes in the world could have been landing overhead or none at all. There was no way of telling.

Mac laughed shortly. "Apparently my instinct was correct. I hadn't really considered you for the job because I wanted you to have the full leave you'd been promised, but when you called last night I had a hunch you were just the man we needed here. We've been having a good deal of difficulty in persuading the lady to cooperate. She gave us an indignant refusal at first, and even after she suddenly changed her mind for reasons that aren't entirely clear—I didn't venture to cross-examine her— she proved very hard to suit in the matter of a working partner." He studied me thoughtfully and spoke without expression. "I suppose it was that intriguingly sinister, ruthless, yet somehow intellectual look that overcame her spinster scruples, where a straightforward display of masculine charm and virility merely offended her. Or maybe she just thought you looked old enough to be reasonably safe."

"Go to hell," I said, "sir."

"Well, you seem to have won the beauty contest, Eric," he said, using my code name to remind me gently that this was an official conversation, and that while many liberties were permitted, there was only one boss. "Matrimony is an essential part of the assignment, you understand. Dr. Mariassy is valuable government property. You can judge how valuable by the caliber of the visitors who came on board today to confer with her and her colleagues. We have obtained permission to use her for bait, but you have to be close enough to her, day and night, not only to watch her but to protect her as well. You can only do that in the character of a lover or husband."

"Sure," I said. "But with two choices, why do we have to pick the legal one?"

"Aside from the fact that she is hardly the type for an illicit love affair, the lady has a career to think of. Neither she nor the government department for which she works wants a scandal attached to her name. After the job is finished, of course, steps will be taken to dissolve the blessed union at no cost to either party. But it must be a genuine marriage while it lasts."

I said, "Well, if she can stand it, I guess I can."

"You will have to," Mac said dryly. "And you will have to be very diplomatic, in private. The rude and arrogant manner she affected today would seem to indicate that she is frightened."

"You think she might panic and pull out, sir? I'll try not to scare her."

"On the other hand," he said, "your performance must carry conviction—both performances. There must be no hint of fakery." He paused. "It's a Taussig operation, Eric. You know what that means. We're not up against amateurs. We can't be too careful."

I frowned. "Taussig? Hell, I thought the old maestro was through. I thought he'd been put out to grass after that Budapest fiasco in fifty-four—well, to a desk in Moscow."

"That was our understanding until quite recently, but apparently it was wrong." Mac glanced at me. "Do you remember the details of what he did in Budapest? I mean, what he almost did in Budapest?"

"Yes, sir," I said. "I wasn't in on it myself, but I was briefed on it afterward. We all were. It was the multiple shadow technique. He had been trying to sell it for years as a substitute for open military action. He had them all covered, all the Hungarian politicians who weren't being properly cooperative. Every doubtful man or woman in public life was shadowed by an agent, trained in homicide who had orders to take his subject out instantly and permanently when the whistle blew. The only trouble was, somebody got nervous and whistled prematurely. Four or five prominent Hungarian citizens died, and there was a big scandal, but the real takeover had to wait for the Russian tanks in fifty-six or -seven, whenever it was."

I grimaced. "You mean he's managed to talk them into letting him try the same thing again?"

"The evidence says so."

"In Pensacola, Florida?" I asked. "Why Pensacola, for God's sake? What's important enough there to warrant the Budapest treatment?"

Mac said, "The exact nature of the Pensacola target is irrelevant. The important thing is that there is one, and that a number of valuable people, Dr. Mariassy included, are in danger, and that we must find Taussig and stop him before he gets all his agents in a position to act."

"Sure," I said. "And just how does Washington plan for me to find him? I gather they don't have his location pinpointed, or there would be no need to use the female scientist for a decoy."

"He was seen in Pensacola a few months ago," Mac said. "That's what drew our attention here. Unfortunately the operative who recognized him—not one of ours—had other business and let it go with a routine report. Taussig has not been spotted since. You'll have to work at it from this end."

"Starting with a marriage ceremony." I opened the book I was still holding and read the name boldly written on the flyleaf in black ink. "'Olivia Eloise Mariassy.' Eloise, for God's sake. What's she a doctor of, anyway?"

"Medicine," Mac said. "Aerospace medicine, to be exact. She is one of a group of government scientists using the facilities of the U.S. Naval School of Aviation Medicine, in Pensacola, and of Eglin Air Force Base up the coast, for a special project. Sometimes, when the missile range at Eglin is inadequate, they call on Cape Kennedy for help. This much you should know. Exactly what the project is, doesn't concern you." He made a wry face. "Or so I was instructed to tell the man who was selected for this assignment."

"Sure," I said. "We're supposed to save the country blindfolded, as always. I suppose it's some kind of a super-retaliation gizmo, or Taussig and his superiors wouldn't be so interested."

"Perhaps," Mac said.

"Aerospace medicine, eh? I'll look it up." I snapped the book shut. "Of course, I won't have much time for research. I'll be playing chess with my bride." This got no reaction from Mac and I said, "What makes us think Taussig's going to take the bait?"

"He may already have taken it," Mac said. "Not Taussig himself, of course. Presumably he was here only to arrange the details of the local surveillance setup; he probably won't risk showing himself here again. He'll control the machinery from a distance as he always does. It's his strength and his weakness. It's the reason we've never been able to reach him; and at the same time it's the reason for the failure of the Budapest operation. He was too far away to take charge when a subordinate panicked." Mac paused. "As far as Pensacola is concerned, we have determined that several of Dr. Mariassy's colleagues have already developed shadows. We are gambling that she has."

"Gambling," I said. "Can't we confirm before we start?"

"Not without the risk of alerting Taussig's man, or woman, if there actually is one assigned to Dr. Mariassy, as we hope. I had the investigators withdrawn for that reason. *You* will determine if she is being shadowed, Eric. If she is, you will lead the shadower to a suitably isolated spot, safe from interference by the police or anybody else, and learn from him, or her, the whereabouts of Emil Taussig."

I listened to the rumble of the big power plant, somewhere far below in the giant ship. "Sure," I said softly. "Sure. Just like that."

Mac nodded. "Just like that."

"It's pretty crude," I said. "There are limits to what can be done with the thumbscrews, sir. If we hit a stubborn one, it could get messy."

Mac's voice was unrelenting. "If you become queasy, you can call in help. I'll have an interrogation team standing by."

"Keep your damn I-team," I said. "My stomach is as strong as anybody's. It just seems to me we could be a little more clever about this."

"Cleverness has been tried," Mac said. "A great many very clever people have been working hard on this without notable results. That is why we were called in. Remember, cleverness is not our specialty, Eric. Other things are."

"Yes, sir," I said; then I frowned. "I thought you said these shadows were recently acquired."

"In Pensacola, yes."

"I see," I said slowly. "Then this local manifestation isn't the first and only—"

"By no means," Mac said. "It was merely selected by us as a suitable point for a counterattack. Do you think I would have been authorized to give you such orders if only one small group of scientists was in danger?"

"It's a big thing, then? Nationwide? Old Taussig is shooting everything in the musket including the ramrod?"

"It is big," Mac agreed. "It was first diagnosed at a base of the Strategic Air Command up north in… well, never mind where. SAC reported that key flight personnel were being watched by enemy agents whose job might be to keep them from reaching their planes under certain circumstances."

"You mean," I said, "if the big bell started ringing?"

"Yes. I regret to say that the report was not, at first, taken very seriously by other government departments. It sounded rather farfetched to anybody who had not heard of Taussig's Budapest venture; and those SAC people have a recognized persecution complex. They are not really happy unless they think somebody is trying to do them in, one way or another."

"Paranoia is the word, sir," I said helpfully.

"Thank you, Eric. Paranoia. Gradually it developed that even allowing for the paranoia of the Strategic Air Command, there was evidence to indicate that something very unpleasant was being planned on a very large scale. One cell was discovered in Washington, D.C. You can imagine the furor this caused, behind tight security, of course. Then Taussig himself was spotted in the country, and somebody did remember Budapest, and the pieces fell into place. Cells are now known or suspected as far apart as San Diego, California, and a certain little-known government activity in Maine. We do not know how many there are. We do not know who is scheduled to die and who is not. This creates a certain amount of panic among various important people who can bravely face the possibility of having millions of people killed by nuclear weapons."

I said, "I know. It's always a little different when it's a man with a gun or knife who's hunting just you."

"As a result," Mac said, "in certain quarters Emil Taussig is no longer looked upon as merely a small, white-haired, Jewish gentleman with an ingenious mind; he is regarded as the devil himself. It is our job to exorcise him. We do not know many of the details of his operation. We do not know if his effort is an independent one, or if there will be concurrent action from overseas to take advantage of the confusion he hopes to create. We do not know," Mac said, "and as far as you are concerned we do not care. Information is the business of other agencies. The only information in which you are interested is: Where is Emil Taussig?"

"Yes, sir," I said.

"You will find him," Mac said, "using any means necessary. When you have found him, you will kill him. Any questions?"

"No, sir," I said. I mean, he'd made it pretty clear.

4

The cocktail lounge of the Montclair Hotel featured a large circular bar built to resemble, vaguely, a circus carousel complete with canopy. For this reason, I guess, it was known as the Carnival Room. All visible seats under the canopy were occupied when I came in, which was fine. It made my choosing a table at the side of the room seem natural, whereas otherwise somebody might have wondered why a lone man would go off in a dark corner by himself instead of sitting at the bar. Somebody might even have wondered later, in the light of developments, if the guy hadn't been expecting company right along.

A waiter won my heart by unhesitatingly supplying a Martini complete with olive, instead of trying to sell me on the virtues of onions, lemon peels, and other garbage. Since the door and who came through it was supposed to hold no interest for me, I concentrated my attention on the assortment of posteriors lined up around the bar. With the evidence before me, I came to the conclusion that it takes a pretty good rump to appear well on a small stool. One female specimen in pink satin, young and unrestrained, was quite intriguing as behinds go, but the rest were no treat to the eye.

I took a drink to celebrate my return to civilian life. Getting off the ship had involved a ride in an old prop trainer that sounded like a bucket of bolts, from the cockpit of which the carrier's three-hundred-yard flight deck had suddenly looked very short. Catapults aren't used to get the propeller jobs airborne. They're supposed to be able to make it on their own, but there had been a moment or two, running out of deck with nothing but ocean left ahead, when I'd wondered if somebody hadn't miscalculated badly.

Braithwaite had lifted us off nicely, however, and set us down on a military field somewhere inland. There I'd inspected some interesting and moderately confidential facilities to make my officer act look good if anybody bothered to trace me this far. Then a car had run us into Pensacola where I changed back into slacks and sports coat, leaving my military identity in the empty apartment with my lieutenant commander's uniform. We'd come roaring back along the beaches in Braithwaite's low-slung Healey, reaching New Orleans a little after dusk.

It had been a complicated damn performance, worthy of the old OSS and similar glamorous organizations. If it had accomplished nothing else, I decided, it had made some service people feel they'd been in touch with great matters of international intrigue. Maybe that was the idea.

I'd got out of the car a few blocks from the hotel.

"Just walk straight ahead, sir," Braithwaite said. "You'll see it on your left. You can't miss it."

"Sure," I said.

"I'm not supposed to ask questions, I know," he said. "But... Ah, hell. Good luck, sir." He held out his hand. It was the first sign of humanity that had peeked through the Naval Academy polish.

I shook his hand and looked down at him for a moment. The sports car in which he sat wasn't much more than knee high. I said, "If you're interested in more of the same, it can probably be arranged on a permanent basis. I'm just passing the word as it was given to me. Personally I'd stick to the Navy if I were you. But you're entitled to know somebody liked the way you handled this."

"Thank you, sir." It was hard to tell in the dark, but I thought his boyish face flushed a little with pleasure. "As for the offer..."

"Don't kid yourself it's all a matter of fancy countersigns and fast driving," I said. "And don't waste your answer on me. The recruiting office..." I told him the number in Washington to call, and gave him a kind of salute. "Happy landings, as we birdmen say."'

Thinking of this now, I felt old and cynical. To cheer myself, I looked for the neat little fanny in pink, but it was gone. Presently I spotted the tight, shiny dress some twenty degrees farther along the curving bar than it had been. My first thought was that the kid had moved to another stool. Then I realized that the great circular contraption, occupying the whole center of the room, was actually rotating like a real merry-go-round, but much more slowly.

I'd been briefed on this earlier, of course, but it had slipped my memory for a moment. Being reminded of it, and seeing it in action, came as kind of a shock, particularly since it was something I wasn't supposed to forget. It was part of our plan. At the same time I became aware that a woman was being seated at the table to my left, only a few feet down the upholstered bench that ran along the wall.

"Waiter," I said, carefully ignoring her, "waiter, either I'm drunk on one Martini or that thing is moving."

There was a quick laugh from the woman who'd just sat down. "It certainly is!" Olivia Mariassy said. "What a dreadful thing to put in a bar! I thought I was intoxicated, too, when I came in here this afternoon and saw it."

This was the approach that had been decided on. I guess Hollywood would have said we were meeting cute. The words were right, but she wasn't the greatest actress in the world, and I don't suppose she'd ever picked up— or been picked up by—a man in a bar before. The laugh was strained and the voice was forced. It wasn't good.

I looked around the way a man might, addressed by a strange woman in a strange place—that is to say, hopefully. After all, I wasn't supposed to know it wasn't Brigitte Bardot who'd sat down beside me. I let my face go disconcerted for a moment before I covered up politely. Dr. Mariassy hadn't altered much since I'd last seen her. Of course, it had been only a few hours, but there are women who can manage a change of clothes and a light application of lipstick in that length of time.

Our scientist lady was still wearing her clumsy tweeds, however. The pulled-back straight hair, the lack of makeup, and the heavily rimmed glasses still gave her the look of a frustrated old-maid schoolteacher. She had made only one change: she'd put on high heels. The table, and the poor light, made it hard to estimate the extent of the improvement, but I got the impression that her legs weren't half bad.

Her smile was pretty awful, however. It obviously hurt her to have to smile at me. Maybe it would have hurt her to smile at anybody. I encouraged myself with that thought.

"Well, it is kind of a strange notion, ma'am," I said politely. "I wonder how long it takes to go around." This was also part of the prepared dialogue. It gave her an opportunity, in line with her scientific character, to suggest breaking out the watches and doing some timing. As the circular bar actually took some fifteen minutes to complete one revolution, we'd be practically old friends by the time this research project was finished and checked—old enough friends, at any rate, for me to buy her a drink and, a few drinks later, ask her to take pity on a lonely Denver character who knew nothing about New Orleans, not even where to find a decent meal.

It was a good enough opening for a pickup romance, but we weren't putting it across. I hoped she could feel it. I hoped she'd have sense enough to stall a little with the cigarette bit, giving me a chance to play gentleman-with-a-match, before she pitched into the act in earnest.

Then I remembered she didn't approve of smoking. I could see her gathering herself to deliver her next line, and I knew it would be about as convincing as a schoolboy's excuse for playing hooky—and a man was watching us from the door.

He made no bones about it. He just stood there regarding us thoughtfully, and I knew he was the one. I didn't have any doubt. I mean, you get so you can spot them, the trained ones, the pros, the men in the same line of work. I don't mean I recognized his face. He was new to me. We didn't have him in the high-priority file, not yet. But he was our man, he had to be. They aren't common. It wasn't likely there'd be two of that species around—besides me, I mean.

He was a big, middle-aged man with a bald head and protruding ears like the symmetrical handles of an ornamental vase, but he wasn't ornamental, far from it. I got an impression of almost spectacular ugliness in the glimpse I allowed myself. I didn't dare look longer. Maybe his instincts weren't as acute as mine. If so, there was a chance that he hadn't spotted me yet; that he was just making note of me in a routine way, as he'd have made note of anybody who made any kind of contact with his real subject, Olivia Mariassy.

There was still a chance, if not a good one. So far she hadn't given herself away hopelessly. A maiden lady intellectual was bound to be a little awkward, adventurously addressing a strange man in a bar. But we couldn't expose him to any more of her phony smiles and memorized dialogue or he'd know the meeting had been planned.

"Excuse me," I said abruptly, and turned away just as she started to speak. "Waiter!"

Rising, I was aware of Olivia's face kind of crumpling. After all, she'd nerved herself to go through with the repulsive performance, and now the horrible man was kicking the script out the door. Well, it could pass for the reaction of a shy woman away from home whose tentative advances had been rudely rejected. I hoped she'd know enough to buy a drink and drink it, as any woman would to cover her confusion, before she ran out. I also hoped she'd remember, then, to go straight to her room and stay there with the door locked as she'd been instructed to do if anything went wrong.

Walking away after paying my bill, I knew it still wasn't good enough. He'd sat down at a corner table; he didn't seem to be looking our way any more, but I knew he wasn't missing a thing. He'd naturally be watching for a plant, a ringer, anything to indicate that his subject was hep and a trap was being set, that a pro was being slipped into the game against him. He wouldn't be watching for it any harder tonight than last night, perhaps, or tomorrow night, but he'd be on his guard always to spot anything out of line. He had to be. His life and his job depended on it.

What was needed, I thought, was a convincing red herring—but maybe a pink one would do. It was a crazy move, but that was a point in its favor, and my luck was in. The kid with the pink satin dress and the nice little rear was still in sight at the revolving bar, and the stool beside her was vacant. She had the defensive look a pretty girl gets in public, waiting for her escort to return from the john. I marched over there, stepped aboard the carousel, sat down, and tossed some money on the bar.

"Martini," I said to the bartender. "Veddy, veddy dry, if you please. Better make it a double."

I threw a wry glance over my shoulder toward Olivia. She had a drink and was sipping it grimly, staring straight ahead, as if she thought everyone in the room was watching. Well, that was still in character. Maybe we'd get by without giving the show away. How we'd make contact again, more convincingly, was a matter I'd give thought to later.

I grinned at the girl beside me. "I have just escaped a fate worse than death," I said. "Heaven preserve me from amorous lady schoolteachers on vacation."

She had black hair and slim bare shoulders and long white gloves. Her eyes were large and dark and framed by rather heavy black eyebrows. She was a nice-looking kid, but she didn't really belong in the bar of the ritzy Montclair, I realized, seeing her at close range. She wasn't exactly shabby, but the tight dress showed minute signs of strain and wear at the seams. The gloves and stockings were beyond reproach, but the pretty pink satin pumps had been walked in and danced in plenty of times before tonight. I wouldn't have been surprised to learn they were getting kind of thin underneath.

She was obviously a kid who had to count her pennies, squeezing just a little more wear out of last year's glamor. She'd got herself a well-heeled date, she'd promoted drinks at the Montclair, and maybe dinner at Antoine's was on the program, too. It would be if she had her way, I thought. She didn't like my butting in one little bit.

"Please," she said stiffly. "I'm sorry. This place is taken."

"Remember me?" I said. "Paul Corcoran, of Denver, Colorado. This is real great, doll! I checked into the hotel last night, knowing nobody in town, I thought. And tonight I drop in here for a drink and look who's sitting here! What about the creep you're with? Can you ditch him?"

She looked at me for a moment longer, long enough to know perfectly well she didn't remember me from anywhere. She looked quickly toward the door marked GENTLEMEN but it remained closed. She glanced toward the bartender.

"I wouldn't," I said softly. "Smile and look down, doll. Coy-like. Then look up again and laugh as if my being here was just about the funniest and nicest thing that ever happened in your young life."

She hesitated and glanced down. Her smile wavered terribly as she saw the little knife in my hand, open, concealed from everyone else by our bodies and the overhang of the bar. The barman put my Martini in front of me, picked up his money and went away, noticing nothing. I reached for the drink left-handed. The kid was still smiling fixedly at the knife.

"Look up at me and laugh now," I said over the rim of the glass. She looked up at me and laughed. Well, you could call it a laugh. "It's four inches long in the blade," I said, "It's very sharp. Take a drink and laugh." She took a drink and laughed. "Did you ever see anybody who'd been opened with a knife?" I asked. "It's very messy, doll. Somebody'll get me, sure, if you yell for help, but they'll be too late. You'll be sitting there holding your guts in place with those nice white gloves, feeling your life run out between your fingers, warm and wet and red. Like, you know, blood."

I was laying it on thick, real colorful stuff. The circular bar was still turning slowly. All around us people were talking and laughing. The kid touched her lips with the tip of her tongue.

"What... what do you want?"

"Look toward the john again and laugh. You're going to ditch your boyfriend now and go with me. We're old friends, remember. Don't forget your purse. Pick it up now." She picked it up mechanically. I said, "The barman is coming this way. Give him the message. Say he's to tell the gentleman that you had to leave but you'll call him in the morning. First take my arm fondly and wink at me as you say it. Now."

It worked. It had happened too quickly for her to think up any tricks, and the barman dealt with drunks and oddballs all night long. He wasn't looking for nuances. Then we were moving out of there, chattering brightly— at least I was chattering brightly—while the slim girl in

pink clung to my arm desperately and smiled and smiled
with panic in her big dark eyes.

The bald man at the corner table didn't look at us once,
all the way to the door. Neither did anyone else except
perhaps Olivia Mariassy, and she'd naturally have some
masochistic interest in watching the man who'd repulsed
her awkward attempt at conversation leaving with a
younger and prettier girl.

5

It was a long way through the lobby to the street door, and my patter had lost a good deal of its spontaneous wit and sparkling originality by the time I got her out on the sidewalk. Then we were walking away from the hotel. It was the old part of New Orleans, with one-way streets barely wide enough for a horse and carriage, and sidewalks barely wide enough for a crinoline. The alley I found was even narrower, just a crack between two tall buildings.

Where I stopped her at last, the night sky was a distant violet-gray strip above us, and the lighted street was a narrow slice of life and hope left far behind, or so it must have seemed to her. When we stopped, she put her back to a blank wall defensively. Her dim face, framed by the midnight-black hair, looked as white as her long gloves.

"What do you think is going to happen to you, doll?" I asked.

She shook her head minutely. "Don't!" she whispered. "Whatever lousy thing you're going to do to me, do it.

Get it over with. Don't tease me. That's dirty."

"I'm not teasing you," I said. "I just want you to know what's going to happen next so you won't go off half-cocked. As soon as I finish talking I'm going to put this knife in your hand. Then, while you're holding the knife, I'm going to kiss you for being a sweet kid and helping me out of a tough spot. Are you ready?"

She stared up at me, startled and confused. Well, that was what I was working for. Now that I'd used her, I had to keep her from telling the police all about it. Being hauled off to jail is one of the things we're not supposed to let happen to us. On the spur of the moment, the romantic mystery-man approach seemed the best bet for silence, short of killing her, which was neither necessary nor desirable.

She licked her lips. "But—"

"Conversation is not required," I said. "Hold out your hand."

I had to reach down and find it and close her fingers about the handle of the knife. I guided the point toward my chest.

"No," I said, "a little to my left, doll. It's tough work shoving a knife through a man's breastbone. That's better. Now make up your mind. All you have to do is push; it'll go in smooth and easy. You'll be surprised how little effort it takes to kill a man. Here comes the kiss."

Moving very deliberately, the way you'd reach for a frightened bird, I took her face in my hands and bent down briefly. Her face was cold and her lips were cold. I felt the knife move very slightly against me, but it never penetrated my coat. I stepped back. She let her hand fall to her side. After a moment I heard a shaky little laugh.

"Mister," she breathed. "Mister, I…" She stopped.

"What's your name?" I asked.

"Antoinette," she whispered. "Antoinette Vail."

"Toni?"

"My friends call me Toni," she said. Her voice was coming in stronger now. "I'll let you know when you qualify. In the meantime… In the meantime, I think Miss Vail sounds very nice, don't you?"

"Yes, ma'am," I said.

We stood for a little while facing each other like that, hearing the sounds of the city all around us; but nothing moved in the dark, narrow alley where we were. She glanced down at the knife in her hand, and looked at me again.

"You scared me," she murmured. "You really scared me! I really thought you… Here, take it!" I took the knife, closed it, and dropped it into my pocket. She was watching me steadily. "What happens if I run?" she asked.

"In here?" I said. "Dark as it is, you'll probably fall over something and ruin your stockings. You'd better walk carefully until you get out where there's some light. If you want to leave."

"If?" she breathed. "*If*? Are you crazy or something? Do you think I—" She stopped.

"Aren't you a wee bit curious? Aren't you intrigued? I must be losing my grip," I said. "Well, then, didn't you have some plans for tonight that I've just shot to hell? Wouldn't you like to have dinner on me—anywhere, any price—and listen to a lot of lies about why I had to do what I did? I'm a fascinating liar, Miss Vail."

"That, I'll believe," she said tartly. "You fascinated me, you and that wicked-looking little slicer. Is your name really Corcoran like you said in there?"

"Hell, no," I said. "It isn't Paul, either. But what do you care? Paul will do for one evening, won't it?"

She said, "I'm not a tramp, Paul. I mean, if that's what you have in mind…"

I said, "Miss Vail, sex is certainly important to me, and you're a lovely girl, but I generally manage to satisfy my requirements without kidnaping young ladies at the point of a knife."

She hesitated, and said with a kind of compulsive honesty, "Of course, I'm not exactly a sheltered virgin, either. You've probably guessed that."

I said, "It's a fascinating subject, but it could be pursued in a warmer place. Did you have a wrap?"

"Yes. It was checked. It isn't the kind of coat you want to flash in a high-class bar. My date will probably take it home with him. God knows what kind of a story I'll have to tell to get it back. He's the jealous type." She hugged herself, shivering. "It is kind of chilly. You said *anywhere?*"

"Yes, ma'am."

"And *any* price?"

"Yes, ma'am."

She hesitated again. Then she laughed and took my

arm. "Well, you asked for it. Antoine's is only a couple of blocks…"

I'd had a hunch it would be Antoine's if she could take her pick. I guess it usually is in New Orleans, although there are supposed to be some newer places with equally good food and atmosphere. Actually, the atmosphere at Antoine's isn't really plush, for all the reputation the place has got. The customers are well-dressed, the waiters know their business and look it, but the dining room itself seems kind of bare and disappointing to anybody who arrives expecting to wallow in the lap of old-fashioned southern luxury. You're supposed to go there to eat, I guess, not to appraise the furnishings.

We had to wait for a table, and the one we got was out in the middle of the floor. The delay bothered me, but I told myself there wasn't really anything else for me to do back at the hotel. Olivia would be all right if she followed instructions, and it was better to let some time pass before we set up another meeting. I might as well be making sure this stray kid I'd involved in the game didn't cause us any official trouble.

"I'd like to go make repairs," Antoinette said after the headwaiter had made us comfortable and departed. "There's something about panic… I feel as if I'd come unraveled, just a little. Do you mind?"

I looked at her across the table. She was really an extremely pretty girl, but pretty wasn't quite the right word. It was an off-beat face, not quite symmetrical, with the heavy black eyebrows almost meeting over the straight little nose. I was betting on those individualistic eyebrows, and on the well-worn satin shoes. She probably wasn't starving, but she was a kid to whom an expensive meal in a fashionable restaurant meant something beyond food; and she was a kid who'd gamble recklessly and high to get it.

"No," I said. "I don't mind."

I watched her go off across the room, slim and straight in her shiny little dress. It was up to her now. There was nothing to be gained by wondering which way she'd turn; I'd know soon enough. There was not much to be gained by wondering what Olivia Mariassy was thinking after her humiliating experience in the Montclair bar, or what the bald man with the craggy face was doing. And there was certainly no profit at all in thinking about a woman who was dead, but I thought about her just the same. We'd had some good times together, Gail and I, even if she'd had too much money and Mac hadn't approved of her. I was going to have to get used to the idea that she wouldn't be around for me to call up when the job was over.

Then Antoinette Vail was returning, her hair very smooth and her lipstick quite perfect, and I rose to manipulate her chair like a gentleman. She smiled up at me as she seated herself.

"Well, there was one," she said.

"One what? Oh, you mean a phone?" I went back and sat down deliberately. I said, "I figured there would be. Did you use it?"

"Of course," she said. "The police don't want to make

a fuss in here, but they'll be waiting whcn we leave. I told them you were armed and dangerous, so they'll probably shoot you down as you step into the street. But we can still have dinner first, can't we?"

"Sure," I said. "All the more reason to enjoy ourselves while we can. Take your choice. The sky's the limit."

She waved the menu aside. "I don't have to look. I want steak and champagne," she said. "It's square, it's corny, and they're not as good with steak here as with fish, but that's what I want. It makes me feel… luxurious. Paul?"

"Yes?"

"How did you know I wouldn't use the phone?"

I said, "You're not a cop-calling girl, Miss Vail. If you were that stuffy and conventional you'd pluck your eyebrows and wear a girdle."

She thought that over for a moment. "Well, I guess it makes sense, vaguely." She had another thought, and looked at me quickly across the table and grinned. "I was going to ask why you picked on me, back there at the Montclair. I guess you've just told me, indirectly, Mr. Paul Sharpeyes Corcoran."

"Sure. You have a beautiful little fanny, Miss Vail. It shows up particularly well on a bar stool. When I had to find a female companion in a hurry, who would I pick from that collection of bulging rumps? Who would any man pick? The corseted lady three stools down? Don't be silly."

Toni laughed and started to speak, but the waiter was hovering nearby, and she changed her mind. We went through the serious formality of ordering dinner. When the waiter had gone again, she leaned forward on her elbows comfortably.

"All right," she said, "let's hear them."

"Let's hear what?"

"The lies. About why you needed a female companion in a hurry. Make them good now."

"Sure," I said. "Well, there's the one about my meeting a married woman for a jazzy New Orleans weekend, and just as we were about to settle down for a drink, who should walk into the bar but her husband? He's a big tough guy. I don't want to tangle with him, and the lady doesn't want any nasty publicity, so I had to act quickly to make it look as if I didn't even know her."

Toni was wrinkling her nose distastefully and shaking her head. "That's not very original. You can do better."

"What's the matter with it?"

"Well, if you were just a weekend Romeo, you'd hardly be flashing a knife like that. And then there's the lady. I suppose you mean the dowdy one in tweed you pointed out as an amorous schoolteacher. She's hardly the type to be stepping out on her husband, if she has a husband; and even if she did want to flip, I can't see you as her partner in sin, Paul. I don't know what you are, but you're a little too smooth to fall for a creep in horn-rimmed glasses."

"Flattery will get you nowhere," I said. "I'm supplying only eats, drinks, and lies. Diamonds and furs you'll have to get elsewhere."

She laughed. "It isn't very nice to call a girl a gold-digger, even just by implication. You might hurt her feelings. No, I don't think much of that story. Try again."

"Well," I said, "how about this? You've heard of the Syndicate; I suppose. Well, I'm on the payroll, see, only I'm hiding out because the fuzz is after me, and I'm running short of the folding ready. So they send my moll with a fresh supply of green, and she's all done up with glasses and a kooky hairdo so nobody'll know her— she's a real dish, normally—but just as she's about to slip me the loot I see a cop come in and I know he's been tailing her. He doesn't know me by sight, and I've made a few changes since the descriptions went out, but I've only got a minute to… No?" I said. "You don't like that one, either?"

"No," she said. "I don't like that one, either."

I sighed. "Lady," I said, "you are very hard to suit. How about this? I'm a government man, see, and I've got a big deal cooking all about spies and saboteurs and stuff, only just as I'm about to make contact with one of my fellow agents, feminine gender, I see a man watching. He's got her spotted, obviously, but there's still hope that I can keep clear if I… No, that won't work."

She was looking at me intently. She touched her lips with her tongue. "Why not, Paul? Why won't it work?"

"Well, hell," I said, "if I were really a government man, I'd have identification, wouldn't I? I'd be just lousy with identification. Did you ever see a government man yet who wasn't ready to flash his buzzer at the drop of a hat?"

"And you haven't got identification?"

"Not the lousiest little bit, doll. I mean, Miss Vail. I'm the most unidentified man you ever saw, Miss Vail."

She said slowly, still watching me, "I think you're one of the cleverest men I ever saw, too, Paul." Her voice was cool. "You want something for nothing, don't you? Well, not for nothing. But for the price of a dinner you want silence and cooperation without committing yourself one tiny little bit. Do you think that's a fair deal?"

I shook my head. "No. Only a damn fool would buy a deal like that. Or a girl who likes steak and champagne and isn't scared of a touch of mystery."

There was a short silence. She reached out and placed her hand on top of mine. "All right," she breathed. "All right. If that's all you're going to tell me."

"I haven't told you anything, Miss Vail. Not a damn thing. Anything you want to guess is up to you, but it's strictly a guess."

"I'm not sure I want you for a friend," she said. "I'm not sure I trust you enough to call you friend." She patted my hand lightly, and sat back, smiling. Everything was settled in her mind, and she murmured, "But I think you'd better start calling me Toni just the same."

6

She lived within walking distance of the restaurant, technically speaking, although I wouldn't have wanted to hike that far on a cool fall night in a thin dress and high heels. But she was still young enough to feel that taxis were corny and walking was reckless and gay— or perhaps she just had some natural reservations about sharing a dark back seat with me and my knife.

Anyway, coming out of the restaurant, I took off my suit coat and put it around her to keep her from freezing, and we hoofed it gaily through narrow streets with shabby old buildings, some with ornamental ironwork on windows and balconies, very picturesque if you like old architecture. I was more interested in the question of whether or not we were being tailed. On foot, in that ancient neighborhood of twisty little lanes, it was hard to tell. If somebody was shadowing us, he was good—but then he would be. That was his business, shadowing. That was why he'd been assigned to Olivia Mariassy in the first place.

Toni's room, apartment, studio, or pad—whatever they called it locally—was up two sights of narrow dusty stairs right under the roof. I couldn't help thinking it would be an oven in a New Orleans summer. She stopped on the landing and gave me back my coat.

"Thanks," she said. She found a key in her purse, unlocked the door, and looked up with her hand on the knob. She spoke in a voice from which all expression had been carefully removed. "Would you like to come in?"

I said, getting into my coat, "That's no way to put it, doll. You're not really concerned with my likes and dislikes, only with my intentions. Sure I'd like to come in. What do you think I am, a eunuch or something? But I'm not coming, thanks just the same."

She smiled faintly, as if she'd proved something about me, and maybe she had. "Why not?" she murmured. "Why the amazing display of self-control?"

"Because if I come in, you'll start wondering if I'm not really figuring you for a sucker or a tramp or both. Hell, you're wondering now, that's why you offered the invitation, isn't it? To see what kind of a slob I really am? But if I treat you with great respect, and just kiss you chastely here at the door and tear myself away, maybe I can make you remember me kindly in spite of the way we met."

She said, watching me, "Just how kindly do you want to be remembered, Paul?"

I said, "To be perfectly honest, I'd rather not be remembered at all, publicly at least. The little man who wasn't ever here, that's me."

"All right," she said. "But hardly little. All right. If that's what you want. I've had a lovely evening after all, and in return I'll follow any instructions you give me. That was the deal. But let's pass up the chaste and respectful kisses, shall we? I don't… don't like playing games with it, if you know what I mean." Her voice wasn't quite even at the end.

I looked at her for a moment, and I had the feeling you sometimes get in the business, that if you'd met somebody at a different time under different circumstances something might have come of the encounter, something you'd rather not think about since it wasn't going to happen. "Sure," I said. "Anything you say, Toni."

She said quietly, "You're a very clever guy, aren't you? The funny thing is, you've almost got me convinced you're a pretty nice guy." She smiled crookedly. "I'll hold that thought as you walk away, Paul Corcoran, or whatever your real name is." There was a little pause while I turned toward the stairs. "Paul?"

I looked back. "Yes, Toni?"

"Good luck," she said softly. "Good luck with whatever you're doing, whoever you are."

Outside I drew a long breath and started up the street thinking it would be swell if wars were fought only by professional soldiers, and undercover operations involved only tough and unscrupulous agents who'd volunteered for the work. I'd used the kid cold-bloodedly to cover my interest in Olivia Mariassy, and she'd repaid me by calling me a pretty nice guy and wishing me luck. She was a bright kid and kind of a brave kid; and she thought she was experienced and sophisticated but she didn't really know the score.

I hoped she'd never learn it through anything I'd done, but there was no way of being sure of that. It's kind of like rabies, except that you don't have to bite anybody to pass it along. Just being seen with them can sometimes be enough. I remembered a case in which a small boy died, never mind where, because he'd politely picked up and returned a small package a lady had dropped—quite accidentally, as it happened, but the people watching her hadn't known that. They'd had to make sure.

Nobody followed me back to the hotel. I was quite certain of that, but the significance didn't strike me until I was crossing the lobby toward the elevators. Then I stopped abruptly with a cold feeling in my stomach, remembering that I'd had no such confidence when we reached Toni's place.

I stood there trying to remember and analyze my reactions. All the way from Antoine's to Toni's the warning signals had been flashing red on the control board. I might not have consciously seen, heard, smelled, or felt anything wrong, but the night had been faintly wrong behind me. From Toni's to the Montclair there had been nothing of the sort. Logic provided the answer: if somebody had followed me to Toni's, he was still there.

It was time for a careful review of the possibilities and their meanings. If our man had really followed me tonight instead of sticking with Olivia, this meant that my red-herring stunt hadn't worked. He'd seen enough of our clumsy meeting to want to investigate me further. And if he'd stuck with Toni instead of tailing me back to the hotel, this meant… I didn't know what it meant.

It was time to think hard and move slowly; it was time for great caution and thorough planning to retrieve, if possible, what could turn out to be a fatal mistake very early in the operation.

It was no time to consider small girls with black hair and unplucked eyebrows. As far as the job was concerned— as far as my duty was concerned—Antoinette Vail had either served a purpose or failed to serve it. Either way, what happened to her now was quite irrelevant.

Still, I told myself, I might learn something by going back, and the man with the craggy face couldn't be two places at once. If he had business with Antoinette, whatever it might be, he was, for the moment, no threat to Olivia. I could indulge my sentiment or curiosity or sense of responsibility a little. I could at least find out what had happened back there, if anything.

The cabbie I got had trouble with one-way streets, and it seemed a long time before I was again standing on the sidewalk in front of the three-story building. There was a light behind the drawn blinds of one of the dormer windows high above. Well, she'd told me she painted. She could have had a midnight burst of artistic inspiration, but it would have been more reassuring if the window had been dark, as if she'd gone right to sleep, tired after an exciting evening.

I went up the stairs fast without taking any of the precautions in the manual except to keep my hand on the little knife in my pants pocket. When I reached the third-floor landing I saw that the door was ajar, and I knew I'd come too late. I drew a long breath, pushed the door aside and stepped into the brightly lit room.

It was a big place under the slanting eaves. At least the floor space was sizable; the ceiling space was less so. A skylight and the window presumably gave illumination by day. Now the light came from a couple of dangling bulbs without shades. There was an easel, but it had been knocked over. There were paints, and some pots of brushes, one of which had been spilled on the floor. There were stacks of canvases on stretchers, several of which had got knocked around. There was a table, stove, refrigerator, and sink; and there were several wooden chairs, some overturned, that looked as if they'd been picked up secondhand like the rest of the furniture.

A cot stood in the corner. It apparently had been shielded from the room by a painted screen, but this had been flung aside. On the cot, face down, lay a small, motionless, terribly disheveled figure, wearing only some torn, shiny pink stuff bunched about the hips and one laddered stocking. The other stocking, the pink satin pumps, and some scraps of undergarments were distributed about the floor with the painting debris. Her long white gloves were laid out neatly on the little, undisturbed table by the door, as if she'd just removed them, starting to undress, when somebody had knocked and she'd turned to answer...

I closed the door behind me and crossed the room. I had no real hope. I didn't speak because I didn't expect her to hear. I put my hand on her shoulder and was more startled than a man of my experience ought to be when she stirred at the touch and sat up abruptly, tossing the tangled black hair out of her eyes.

"You," she whispered. "*You!*"

"Me," I said, withdrawing my hand.

"You came back," she whispered. "Well, I hope you're satisfied! He did a good job, didn't he? You must be very pleased! You've proved something, haven't you? I don't know what, but something. Oh, God, and I thought you were nice. *Nice!*"

After a little, indifferently, she pulled up a handful of the wrecked satin dress to cover her breasts, but not before I'd seen the ugly bruises. She had an incipient black eye and a cut lip. There was blood on her chin from the cut. But she was alive, I told myself. At least she was alive.

She licked her lips, touching the cut gingerly with her tongue. Her eyes, under the thick black brows, hated me.

"You creep!" she breathed. "You disgusting *creep*, with your knife and your kiss and your smooth, smooth line... Oh, you were good, you were great, Mr. Corcoran. You had the little girl feeling all romantic and warm inside. Hell, there were tears in her eyes as she watched you go away down the stairs. And then the other man came, the one for whom you'd really been putting on the show all the time. Isn't that right? You didn't really give a damn about me; you were just using me. All the time it was an act for his benefit, wasn't it? In case you don't know, his name is Kroch, Karl Kroch. He told me to call you and tell you. Well, you're here, so I'm telling you. Now get out of here!"

"Kroch," I said. "Why did he want you to tell me?"

"How should I know why?" she demanded. "You're the clever one. You figure it out."

"Are you all right?" I asked.

Her eyes widened scornfully. "Why, I'm fine," she said savagely. "I'm great, Mr. Corcoran, don't I look it? I'm marvelous. I've just been slapped all over my studio. I've been tossed on my bed and had most of my clothes ripped off by a gorilla who didn't really care any more about my body than if I'd been a store-window dummy. He just... just violated me because it was the lousiest thing he could think of to do to me short of killing me. He said this would let you know he meant business and couldn't be stopped. He said when the time came he'd act and to hell with you. He said if you had any objections he wouldn't be hard to find. He said this would tell you the kind of man you had to deal with."

"Karl Kroch," I said.

"That's the name," she said. "A real crazy goon. And he can come back any time and go through the same routine all over again, and I'll just be happy because he isn't you! Why... why I really *liked* you. And you set me up for *that!*" She drew a harsh breath. "Now, if you've had your eyeful, get out of here! P-please get out of here!" Her voice faltered on the last sentence.

I asked, "Do you want a doctor?"

She shook her head. "No. He'd just ask a lot of dumb questions. I... I'm all right. I told you before I wasn't a sheltered virgin. I've had it rough before. Maybe not this rough, but rough. I'm all right. Just go away, will you?" She was silent for a moment. "Paul."

"Yes?"

"You might at least have warned me! You might have let me know what you were getting me into. You might have told me the kind of people... He had a face like Mount Rushmore before they carved presidents on it. It never changed. He didn't get any bang out of mussing me up or even... even taking me. It was like he was a machine just programmed to... Is that the way you are, Paul? Inside? Behind that humorously satanic look that makes a girl feel she's found somebody, well, dangerous but nice. Just another machine with a different face? One machine labeled Kroch. One machine labeled Corcoran. Playing some kind of lousy, mysterious game. And a naïve little softhearted sentimental kook named Vail, caught in the middle!"

I said, "If there's anything I can do—"

"I told you. You can get out of here!"

"Sure." After a moment, I started to turn away.

"You don't have to worry," she said behind me. "It's still a deal. It's a lousy, rotten deal but I agreed to it and I'll stick to it. I won't call the police and interfere with your crummy business, whatever it is. I won't talk." Her voice was hard. "But on second thought, there *is* something you can do. You can pay for the damage. My wardrobe is kind of limited. I've got plenty of jeans with paint on them, but I don't have so many dresses I can afford to have them torn up."

I took out my wallet and went back to her and put some bills on the bed beside her, all I had with me except the small stuff. She picked them up and counted them and looked up quickly.

"And just what do you think you're paying for, Mr. Corcoran, an easy conscience?" she demanded scornfully. "You've been around, you know perfectly well this cheesy little satin number didn't cost any two hundred dollars. It was thirty-nine fifty on sale last year. Ten bucks will cover the rest. The bruises will heal, and I don't put a price on my self-respect or whatever you want to call *that*. Here!"

She held out three of the four fifties I'd given her. There was nothing to do but take them. I looked down on her small, hurt, hating face for a moment. I tried to reassure myself with the thought that the fate of nations and the lives of important people were at stake, and that what happened to one little girl wasn't really important, but I didn't try to sell the idea to her, perhaps because I wasn't sure I bought it myself.

I turned and walked to the door. A faint sound made me look back. She was again lying face down on the bed. Maybe she was crying. I couldn't be sure. The one thing I could be sure of was that I wasn't the man to console her. I paused by the door to slip the three fifties under her gloves before I went out. After all, by the looks of the place, she'd had a lot of stuff ruined in here besides a dress.

Maybe I was trying to buy an easy conscience, as she'd charged. At a hundred and fifty bucks it would have been a bargain if it had worked, but it didn't.

7

But it was no time for sentimental luxuries like consciences. They're not supposed to be part of our equipment, anyway. I got back to my hotel room as quickly as possible and called Washington by way of Denver, Colorado, since that's where I was supposed to be from and communications had been set up accordingly. I was put through to Mac right away.

"Emergency, sir," I said. "How fast can you make contact with our lady genius? I'd rather not call her directly if I can help it, at this point in the proceedings."

"It shouldn't take more than a couple of minutes," Mac said. "What is the message?"

"Tell her to make sure her door is locked. There's a wild man loose. I have some other instructions I want you to forward, but they can wait while you get the electrons moving."

"Very well. Hold on."

Waiting, I happened to glance across the room. It was

a mistake. The mirror above the dresser caught my eye. The guy who looked back at me wasn't a nice guy. There wasn't anything humorously satanic about him, either. He just looked plain mean.

"They are setting it up." Mac's voice was back in the phone, crisp and business-like. "You'd better bring me up to date while we wait."

"Yes, sir," I said. "We goofed the contact earlier in the evening. The Mariassy is no Lady Barrymore, to say the least. She gave the show away, or something did, although I broke up the performance when I saw we weren't putting it over. Now, if she's followed orders, she's in her room waiting to hear from me, according to the emergency routine we set up. The further instructions I want you to pass along are that she's to go down to the bar in exactly half an hour—that'll give me time to look around a bit and get into position to cover her. She's to enter the lounge looking moody and disconsolate as if her New Orleans vacation wasn't panning out too well. I'll come in shortly. I'll walk up and offer to buy her a drink by way of apologizing for my past rudeness. Presently more liquor will flow. She will absorb her share, at first, with dignified restraint and reluctance, later more willingly to the point of vanishing inhibitions. Seduction will follow. At least it will seem, to follow, to anyone watching. How's that call coming? I'd like to be sure she has sense enough to keep her door shut like she was told."

"They'll ring when they're ready." Mac was silent for

a moment. I sensed his disapproval. "Isn't this a little obvious, Eric? Besides not being quite in line with the agreement we made with the lady and her department? We promised to preserve her reputation, remember?"

"Also her life," I said. "Things have happened, sir, and I'd like to be in a position to keep a better eye on her. Assure her that her virtue will remain intact and that her reputation will be restored by the matrimony route very shortly. We just haven't got time to make the preliminary sparring look as refined and proper as we'd planned, and it may not matter anyway. Please switch on the recorder."

I heard a click. He said, "Recording. Go ahead, Eric."

"Male, forty-five give or take five. Those rocky faces are hard to judge," I said. "Say a hair under six feet. Say two-twenty give or take five. A lot of shoulder. Some paunch. Pretty much a skinhead. What hair there is, is kind of grizzled. I never got close enough to make the eye color. Nose big, bony, has been broken. Ears protruding, a regular jughead. The name he gives out is Karl, Karl Kroch. They shouldn't have any trouble running him down. Everything about him says pro. End of description."

"Hold on again... All right, he's being checked."

"What about Mariassy?"

"They're having a little trouble with the circuits."

"Well, I'll give them another couple of minutes, and then I'd better warn her direct and to hell with our cover. This Kroch has worked over one female tonight; I don't want to give him a crack at another."

"Tell me what's happened," Mac said, and I told him. When I was finished, he was silent for a moment. I could visualize him frowning. He said at last, "That isn't good. Obviously your cover is thoroughly blown already, at least as far as this Kroch is concerned, and he would seem to be the audience you were playing for. What about the Vail girl? Could she be implicated?"

"It's hard to see how, sir," I said. "She could hardly be a plant. I picked her at random out of a whole bar full of people."

"Well, she's obviously involved now. And even if she's completely innocent, she can make trouble for us if she decides to go to the authorities. It's always embarrassing having to clear up these things through official channels, and any publicity right now would be a serious handicap to the whole operation."

I said, "She won't go near the police."

"So she told you. But women have been known to change their minds, waking up in the morning bruised and disfigured, wondering how they can explain their humiliating appearance to friends and neighbors."

I said, "She won't talk, sir. I'll bet money on it. But if you want to put a local man to watching her, okay. He can at least see that nobody bothers her again."

Mac hesitated. "You seem to have been impressed by this young girl, Eric."

I glanced at the mean-looking hombre in the mirror.

I said, "Hell, I threw her to Kroch deliberately, as it

turned out. I just feel kind of responsible for her now. She's a good kid."

"Good or bad, a little surveillance won't harm her. And it may give us advance warning in case she doesn't live up to your high expectations. Now what about the man?"

I glanced at my watch. Not as much time had passed as I'd thought. I told myself Mariassy was safe enough if she followed instructions. Unlike Toni Vail, she knew she was involved in a dangerous game. If she stuck her neck out contrary to orders, it was her own damn fault.

"Karl Kroch?" I said. "I only saw him once. As I told you, sir, he's got the earmarks of a pro. And he does a real smooth job of tailing for such a big man: you'd never know he was there. But he talks too much. All that stuff he told Toni, including his name, for God's sake! And his warning to me that he's going to act when the time comes and to hell with me. That's schoolboy stuff. Either he's a screwball with delusions of grandeur who really thinks he can scare me off by roughing up girls, or he's deliberately putting out a lot of phony bluster and playing a real cagey game underneath. But if so, what is it?"

Mac said, "It's possible he's being clever, of course. However, you know how those big hard men sometimes get after years of success in the business. They start thinking the rules are not for them—they don't have to be careful like lesser agents; they can run right over any opposition. They are superhuman and practically invisible, they think. Shortly thereafter they are either killed or put away quietly to dream their Napoleonic dreams in locked and padded rooms. Mr. Kroch seems to be displaying most of the symptoms."

"Maybe," I said, unconvinced. "But I never like to act on the assumption that a man is crazy until I actually see him foaming at the mouth, sir."

"He seems to have worked up a pretty good lather tonight," Mac said, "judging by the Vail girl's report. And we can be glad of it. His behavior gives us a chance of retrieving what might have been a complete disaster. Under ordinary circumstances, once he spotted you, a man in Kroch's position would simply have disappeared and notified his superiors to send in an unknown replacement. As it is, overconfident, he apparently intends to stay right on the job covering Dr. Mariassy in spite of you. He has even served notice that if he gets the signal to act he will execute it right under your nose. As a result of this bravado, he is still available to you if you act quickly, before he has time to reconsider."

"Yes, sir," I said. "That's another reason I decided to speed up the romance time table."

Mac was silent for a moment. "Since Kroch already has you spotted, there would seem to be hardly any reason left for the amateur theatrics."

"We've got to be doing something plausible while we're getting him out of town to where we can take him," I said. "I don't know New Orleans well enough to pull anything here; I'd probably wind up behind bars. And Kroch is acting very funny and kind of obvious, as if he were really trying to draw attention to himself. What if there's somebody else to do the dirty work, and big, blustering, loudmouthed Kroch is just a decoy?"

"In that case, the other agent will have been warned about you by Kroch. Your performance with Dr. Mariassy will not deceive him, either. And we are not interested in identifying every possible agent involved. All we want is one man who will talk. One man who will lead us to Taussig."

I said, "God knows I'm not yearning to get drunk and disorderly with our tweedy intellectual, sir, let alone marry her, even in name only. But until I know exactly what's going on, I'd rather stick to the original plan with minor modifications. It may still fool somebody, who knows?"

"Well, maybe you're right," Mac conceded. "On second thought, it's never wise to drop a cover hastily, particularly when the opposition is acting in a peculiar manner. Very well, I—" He stopped. I heard a phone ringing in the upstairs office some fifteen hundred miles to the north and east of where I sat. "Just a minute. This is probably the call we're waiting for."

I sat on the bed and looked at the wall and thought about a small, hurt, disheveled girl lying face down on a rumpled bed in a wrecked room. Then I thought of a burning car and a shape under a blanket and a single silver slipper. I heard Mac pick up the phone. When he spoke, his voice held a note of urgency.

"Eric."

"Yes, sir."

"We cannot reach Dr. Mariassy. She has ostensibly

retired and left orders at the hotel desk to the effect that she is not to be disturbed. Without causing comment, it wasn't possible to determine by phone whether the voice that gave the orders was male or female."

"Oh, Jesus!" I said. "I knew I should have gone straight to her. Well, to hell with the meet-cute act, I'm on my way."

8

Olivia Mariassy had a room on the third floor, two below mine. I used the stairs. Nobody seemed interested in where I was going. Nobody seemed to be hanging around the corridor in front of number 310, either. I had the feeling I was in the clear, but I didn't take time to make sure. I just went right up to the door and knocked.

A feminine voice responded promptly. "Who is it?"

I drew a long breath. I guess I'd been really worried. After a moment of relief, I started to get angry. Our tame scientist was still alive and, from the calm sound of her voice, unharmed, but apparently she expected me to shout my name and business through the panels; and what the hell was the idea of having the desk refuse to call her, anyway?

"The password is flattop," I said softly, "like in aircraft carrier."

"Oh."

There was a little pause; then the door opened. She was

still fully dressed in her tweed suit. Her only concession to the lateness of the hour was that she'd unbuttoned her jacket. She was fastening it up again primly as she stood there. She even had her shoes on, although I would have been willing to bet she hadn't had them on a minute earlier. No woman, no matter how intellectual and proper, sits and reads late at night in high heels.

That's what she'd been doing when I knocked: reading. A light burned over the big chair in the corner, and she was holding a fat book with her forefinger marking the place. The title, I noted, was *The Algebra of Infinity,* whatever that might mean.

Standing there facing me she looked, I thought, like a not unhandsome spinster librarian about to ask me sternly why I couldn't get into the habit of returning my books on time.

"What are you doing here?" was what she really asked. "I mean, is this wise, Mr. Corcoran? After all, we're not supposed to be acquainted yet, are we? That abortive incident in the bar hardly constituted an adequate introduction."

"Are you all right?" I asked, watching her face. "Are you alone in there?"

She looked startled first and then indignant. "Alone? Of course I'm alone! What do you mean?"

I relaxed. It was obvious from her behavior that nobody was holding a gun on her from a hidden corner and telling her what to say. I pushed past her. The room was empty. So were the closet and bathroom. I came back to face her and reached out to shove the hall door closed.

"Now," I said, "what's the big idea, Doc?"

"I don't understand."

"I mean the phone bit. We tried to reach you. No go. Somebody had told the desk you didn't want to be disturbed. Naturally, knowing that under the circumstances—particularly after the bar scene—you'd be much too smart to cut yourself off from us, in fact you'd be waiting for me to call, we got just a little concerned."

Her hand went to her mouth, ingénue fashion. It was an oddly girlish gesture for a woman with her severe appearance. "Why, I never thought! I guess I'm not a very good secret agent, Mr. Corcoran. I'm terribly sorry. I just… well, it was a personal matter. Somebody with whom I didn't want to speak."

"Personal," I said. "This is a hell of a time for personal matters, Doc."

"People with medical degrees rarely like to be called Doc, Mr. Corcoran." She was her stiff, precise self once more. "And you are hardly in a position to criticize, after the way you left our business unfinished this evening to chase after that child in pink—leaving me, I must point out, in a very humiliating position. I remember your saying on the ship that you ran after women, but I didn't realize it was compulsive!"

I stared at her. "You don't think I went off with the kid for fun, for God's sake!"

"What else could I think?" Her voice was cold. "And I must say I'm disappointed in your taste, Mr. Corcoran.

That shiny little dress, so tight, so short, so bare. Why do the little tarts all feel it's charming to overflow their clothes like that, all arms and legs and naked shoulders?"

I said, "Never mind my taste, or hers. That little tart, as you call her, has just been beat up and raped because of us. You might keep it in mind while you criticize her clothes. You might also keep it in mind the next time you feel like shutting off your phone for personal reasons. This isn't a friendly rubber of bridge, you know. Just what were your personal reasons?"

"I told you. Just somebody I didn't want bothering me with calls." She wasn't thinking of this at all. She was looking at me with shock and disbelief. "*Raped?*"

"It's a technical term for sexual intercourse achieved by violence. Just who is this guy you don't want to talk to?"

"Never mind," she said evasively. "It's a private matter. It has nothing to do with this. Why was the girl... raped?"

"Apparently as a gesture of spite and defiance," I said. "I was using her to create a diversion and somebody saw through it and took this way of telling me what he thought of my tricks. Anyway, that's one explanation. There may be others."

Olivia was frowning. "Then you didn't leave me just because—" She stopped.

"Just because I suddenly got hot pants for the kid? Not exactly," I said. "We were being watched, Doc, by a man who wasn't buying what we were selling. I thought I could confuse the issue, but the idea backfired."

"Then... then I owe you an apology."

"I'd rather have some dope on this guy who's been pestering you on the phone."

She shook her head. "I assure you, it's completely irrelevant, Mr. Corcoran. You say we are being watched? Well, that's what we hoped, isn't it? That was the reason for the great dramatic effort. So you've already identified the man we're after?"

"Yes, I've identified him," I said grimly. "The only trouble is, he's identified me, too. He's behaving very peculiarly, however, so until we get him figured out we'll go right on with the show as if nothing had happened." I looked at her for a moment. It was obvious that she had no intention of answering questions and we were wasting time, so I said, "I'm leaving now. The sooner I get out of here the better; maybe we can still salvage this act. You will lock your door and call the desk right away and tell them to put through any calls. Then you will give me twenty minutes to check around outside and get set to watch over you properly. If I call in the meantime and tell you to stay put, you will stay put come hell or high water. You will not open to anyone who doesn't give this knock." I rapped lightly on the back of a chair, three and two. "You will not leave this room for anyone who gives you instructions over the phone, regardless of who they claim to be. If it takes a week, you'll wait right here until somebody comes along who gives the proper knock. You've got water in the bathroom and people have lived for months without food, I'm told. Do I make myself clear?"

She licked her lips. "All right, Mr. Corcoran. And if you don't call, what do I do when the twenty minutes are up?"

I told her. She didn't like it, but my shocking news and the fact that she'd misjudged me had apparently rattled her, and she didn't protest very hard. I went out and waited until I heard the lock set behind me; then I went down to a pay phone and called Mac to let him know no female scientists had been lost or damaged. I told him how the situation stood. Then I made a check of the premises and found no sign of Kroch, which didn't necessarily mean anything. He seemed to be good at leaving no sign when he didn't want any left.

Olivia came out of her room in exactly twenty minutes by the clock. There was something to be said for working with scientific personnel after all. I watched her descend the stairs and cross the lobby, gave her a minute or two in the lounge, and went in after her.

She'd taken the table I'd had earlier, over by the wall. I hesitated, discovering her there, and went over.

"Well, did you ever learn how long it took, ma'am?" I asked.

She looked up, startled, and frowned at me in a puzzled way. "How long?"

"The bar. To go around."

"Oh," she said quickly. "Oh, you're the man... I didn't recognize you."

"I was sorry to have to run off like that, earlier, but I saw somebody I didn't know was in town. Do you mind if I sit down, ma'am?"

"Why," she said, "why no. Not at all. Please do."

"We could clock it now," I said. "That fat man. We can see how long it takes before he gets back in front of us. Let me get you a drink…"

Well, you can take it from there. We went through the standard getting-acquainted routine. I trotted out the story of my coming from Denver and being a newspaperman there, and she told me about coming from Pensacola and doing something scientific and secret she wasn't allowed to talk about. She could, however, tell me, she said, if I was interested, about some phenomena she'd encountered in her work that weren't classified. Take weightlessness, for instance…

A couple of drinks later we were still talking weightlessness. "Of course, now that we've actually put men into space, we no longer have to simulate this particular situation, we can study it in actual practice," she said. She remembered something and looked up quickly. "Oh, damn, our fat man is gone! The experiment is ruined, I'm afraid, Mr. Corcoran."

"Let's try the brassy-blonde lady with the silver foxes. She looks pretty permanent; maybe she'll stay for a complete go-round. How about another drink?"

"Well, I shouldn't," she said a little uncertainly. "I'm afraid I'm just talking shop and boring you terribly. Well, maybe I *will* have just one more, if you don't think I'll be too intoxicated. I'm trusting you to keep track and not let me disgrace myself. Although I'm not at all sure you're a trustworthy person, Mr. Corcoran."

She was putting on a much better show than she had earlier in the evening. By this time she had the flushed, bright-eyed, vivacious, faintly disorganized look of the unpracticed lady drinker who's overdoing it. Anybody could tell her inhibitions were taking an awful beating. On more intimate terms now, we discussed my trustworthiness, or lack of it, at length and in laughing detail. I looked up to see the waiter standing by the table.

"One more of each," I said, shoving the empty glasses toward him.

"I'm sorry, sir." He gestured toward the bar, where the last man on duty was shutting up shop. We were alone in the lounge.

"Oh, dear," Olivia said, "Are they closing up? Do we have to go? We never did learn how long it takes to go around."

"The bar?" said the waiter. "It takes about fifteen minutes, ma'am."

I paid the bill, rose, and helped Olivia to get around the table the waiter pulled away from the bench.

She held my arm to steady herself. "I'm afraid I'm just a wee bit inebriated, Mr. Corcoran. It's a very interesting experiment. I've always wanted to try it—in the interest of science, of course—but I've always been afraid of making a fool of myself. Am I?"

"What, making a fool of yourself?" I said. "Not yet, Doc, but I'm still hoping."

"Now I'm sure you're not to be trusted!" She laughed, and stopped laughing. "Do I look all right? My hair isn't coming down, is it? I look like an utter witch with my hair down. Not that I'm any beauty with it up, don't think I have any illusions along those lines. It's really very kind of you to… She stopped and drew a long breath, leaving the sentence unfinished. We were out in the lobby and they were locking the doors of the Carnival Room behind us. Olivia drew herself up and patted her hair, facing me. When she spoke again, her voice was brisk and business-like and sober. "You've been very considerate, Mr. Corcoran, listening to the boring prattle of a lonely woman. No, you don't have to see me to my room. I'm perfectly all right."

I cleared my throat. "Well, I was kind of thinking of *my* room, ma'am. It seems a pity to break this up. I've got a bottle in my suitcase. We could continue the scientific experiment, er, in private."

It was funny. We were acting—with some help from the drinks, of course. We were going through the age-old motions of the pickup for the benefit of anyone who might be watching. And yet the tight, embarrassed little silence that followed my suggestion was real enough. Olivia's laugh was slow to come, and strained when it did come.

"Oh, my dear man!" she murmured. "My dear man! Are you going to flatter the unattractive lady intellectual by making a real pass? Isn't that carrying the Good Samaritan act pretty far?"

"We're going to have to do something about that inferiority complex, Doc," I said. "I don't like to hear a good-looking woman running herself down."

"You know I'm drunk, deliciously drunk, and you're deliberately taking advantage of a foolish, intoxicated... Do I really want to be seduced, Mr. Corcoran?" I didn't say anything. We faced each other for some long seconds; then she laughed again softly and recklessly. "Well, why not?" she asked, taking my arm again, in an intimate way. "Why not?"

We stood very close in the elevator for the operator's benefit; we didn't speak because it wasn't necessary. We got out at the fifth floor, turned left, and walked arm in arm to my door. I put the key into the lock. With the door opening under my hand, I turned to look at my companion.

There was something I'd forgotten. I wondered if she had. There was one affectionate little scene still to be played for our public, if we had one, before we could escape into the privacy of the room and be our cool, distant and professional selves once more.

I saw a sharp little glint in Olivia's eyes, and I knew she'd been wondering if I'd try to leave this particular chore undone. I reached out, took the glasses gently from her nose, folded them, and tucked them into the breast pocket of her jacket while she stood quite still facing me. Then I kissed her. It wasn't too difficult. The woman wasn't actually revolting, and I was moderately tight myself. She wasn't too clumsy, either. At least she knew where the noses went.

I had time to be a little surprised at this. After all, she didn't give the impression of having had much recent practice, if she'd ever had any. Then I sensed somebody behind me, and, releasing her, I turned, ready, and caught a glimpse of a man's face that might have been handsome if it hadn't been contorted with anger. It wasn't a face I'd ever seen before.

That changed the picture. I'd been expecting Kroch. I had to make a snap decision and I made it. Instead of going into action, I just stood there flat-footed and let a fist catch me on the jaw and knock me against the doorjamb. Another fist to my stomach doubled me up. A third fist—well, maybe my count wasn't quite accurate, maybe the guy had only two but it seemed like more— took me alongside the head and knocked me down.

9

It took a bit of doing, of course. No man really likes to be used as a punching bag in front of a woman, even if she isn't quite Sophia Loren. There was even a certain risk, but an attacker who really means business seldom wastes his time and effort with the fists. You get so you can sense when there is real danger, and when the worst that can happen is getting your block knocked off in an amateurish way.

A moment after I'd hit the hall carpet, Olivia was kneeling beside me. Her hand touched my face, but her words weren't addressed to me.

"That was brave!" I heard her cry. "To attack a man from behind, without warning! That's just what I would have expected from you, Harold!"

"You were going into his room!" Harold, whoever he was, had a fine baritone, with indignant overtones.

"And why not? It wouldn't be the first time I'd gone into a man's room, would it? Not quite the first!"

"Look at you!" he cried, ignoring this. "Letting a cynical reporter—oh, I asked about him at the desk—ply you with liquor until you can hardly stand and bring you up here! He was laughing at you, Olivia, couldn't you see? He just thought it was an amusing way to spend an evening. It meant nothing to him, nothing at all."

She said fiercely, "That's right, nothing! No more than it meant to you. You're a fine one to criticize other men's motives!"

"Olivia—"

"Do you think I didn't know what he was doing?" she demanded. "All right, so it amused him to be charming to the mousy lady scientist. Maybe it amused me to play up to him! Maybe I thought it would be entertaining to deliberately let a slick, experienced character like that get me drunk and... and lure me to his room for immoral purposes. After all, I seem to be susceptible to slick characters, and what does it matter now? At least he was honest, Harold. At least he said nothing about love!"

I would have liked to listen to them longer, but they were being pretty loud and somebody in a neighboring room might get tired of the noise and call the manager. I'd learned about as much as I could hope for. I stirred, therefore, groaned, and opened my eyes. I sat up dazedly. Olivia helped me. I looked up at the man who had slugged me.

He was in his late twenties or early thirties with a roughhewn touch of Lincoln or Gregory Peck about the physiognomy, carefully cultivated. It was obvious that regardless of what might have come between them lately, he and Olivia were born to be soulmates. His tweeds were every bit as tweedy as hers, and his glasses were no less thick and black in the rims. They gave him a sincere and earnest look.

"If you'd only let me explain!" he was saying.

She wasn't looking at him any more. "Are you all right, Paul?" she asked.

"You're making a terrible mistake," Harold protested. "If you'd only listen, darling! You completely misunderstood what you heard in the office that day. Miss Darden and I were only—"

She didn't turn her head. "Haven't you done enough? Do you have to wake the whole hotel, too? You can't persuade me there was any misunderstanding. You and your nurse made it all perfectly plain. I could hear you clear out in the waiting room, every word. You should really close the door before you indulge in private jokes with your employees, Harold!"

"It wasn't what you thought—"

"I heard my name quite plainly." Her voice was harsh. "The GLP complex, you called it, meaning grateful lady patient. Apparently it's a recognized syndrome and one of which unscrupulous medical practitioners sometimes take advantage, as you did. Well, this lady patient is no longer grateful, Dr. Mooney. Good-bye!"

She helped me to my feet. The guy was still standing there, still protesting, but she never looked at him. She just led me into my room and closed the door behind us.

Then she turned and locked it carefully. Finally she faced me again and raised both hands to her hair, smoothing it back from her temples wearily.

"Phew!" she said softly. "Well, there you have my private reason for not receiving telephone calls, Mr. Corcoran. I hope you approve of the performance I put on for him."

"A little more practice and we'll have you in the movies," I said.

I stepped up to the door and listened. There was no sound outside. Presently I heard the elevator doors clang shut far down the hall. I turned back to Olivia to find that she'd gone over to sit in the big chair with which my room, like hers, was provided.

"Dr. Harold Mooney," I said. "Doctor of what?"

"Obstetrics and gynecology," she said. "He's a specialist in women's diseases. Also, I'm afraid, in women. He's quite a specimen, isn't he? Genus Casanova, species phony. He's come all the way from Pensacola to plead for forgiveness, he says, but what he's *really* frightened of is that I'll make a scandal and ruin his profitable practice. As if I'd want to let people know what a fool I've been!"

She drew a long, uneven breath, fished for her glasses in her pocket, and put them back on. After a moment, she unbuttoned her jacket, unfastened the snug round collar of her silk blouse, sighed with relief, leaned back comfortably, and stuck her legs out in front of her, a little apart. Her attitude was mildly defiant as if she was aware that this pose was neither graceful nor ladylike and to hell with it. She looked up and saw me rubbing my jaw.

"I thought you people were supposed to be able to take care of yourselves," she murmured with a touch of malice.

I said, "What did you want me to do, pitch him out of a fifth-floor window with a judo throw, or crack a couple of vertebrae with a karate chop to the neck? Besides leaving us the problem of disposing of a body, those are hardly techniques you'd attribute to a dissipated lecherous Denver reporter. Besides, there's the possibility that we may want the guy alive."

She frowned quickly. "What do you mean?"

I looked down at her. Her relaxed posture allowed a lot of leg to show. There was even some lingerie on display; a nice bit of cream-colored slip with darker, coffee-colored lace, pretty and provocative and completely out of character—but then, so was a love affair with a handsome doctor. Somebody had obviously slipped, digging out her background; she'd managed to keep some things well concealed. There was obviously more to Dr. Olivia Mariassy than her plain, tweedy, unpromising exterior had seemed to indicate.

"Where did you meet this guy?" I asked.

"In his office. Although we're kind of attached to the Naval Air Station and use their facilities, we don't officially rate attention from the Navy doctors, and being a doctor myself I detest people who try to scrounge free medical service they're not entitled to. Later, I met Dr. Mooney at a cocktail party in town. He remembered me, which was flattering. Most men don't, as a person, although they may remember me as a scientist." She spoke in a dry, detached voice. "We talked about medicine and other things. We had dinner together that night and other nights. You can guess the rest."

"Sure." I crossed the room to the phone, and activated the New Orleans-Denver-Washington circuits for the second time that night. "Never mind switching me upstairs," I said to the girl when I got the number. "Just have them run a fast check on Mooney, Harold—M.D. in obstetrics and gynecology and don't ask me how to spell it. Home base, Pensacola, Florida. Let me have it here in the morning, whatever you can get at once; in the meantime tell them to put somebody to really digging for dirt. Check his home, his office, everything. Any word on Karl Kroch yet?"

There wasn't, which was odd. Generally they can run down a man with a record in the business pretty fast, and I was willing to bet Kroch's record was long and gaudy. I hung up. Olivia hadn't moved.

"Karl Kroch?" she said. "Is that the man—"

"The one who was watching us in the bar downstairs, earlier this evening. The one who was so mean to the little girl in pink. The one we wanted, I thought. Now I'm not so sure."

"Because of Harold?" Her eyes followed me as I came back across the room. "You're wrong, Mr. Corcoran. I can see your line of reasoning, of course, but you're wrong."

I said, "We put on an act, Doc. We met cute, we got drunk cute, we indicated we were going to make love cute, just to see who'd be interested. Well, there were distractions, but a fish finally took the bait, didn't he? Your friend Mooney had obviously been watching us off and on. He admits he even checked on me at the desk."

She was still lying back in the big chair, relaxed and surprisingly careless about what showed and what didn't, considering where she was and what she was. I reminded myself that I was no longer quite sure what she was. The longer this night went on, it seemed, the less sure I was about anything.

"It's plausible," she said thoughtfully, "it's plausible, but it's wrong. The man who's watching me is supposed to be a trained professional killer, isn't he? Well, Harold couldn't commit that kind of crime if his life depended on it. He hasn't got the nerve, Mr. Corcoran. Swinging a fist at a man who isn't looking is just about his limit. He's a... a handsome phony. I know." She grimaced. "*Now* I know."

I said, "Still, he apparently made a point of getting acquainted with you in Pensacola. He followed you here. We can't ignore him just because you think he's a lightweight. It's standard procedure, Doc, for an agent to act dumber and more scared than he is."

"Well, I'm sure you're mistaken." She sighed, giving up the argument, and surveyed the room lazily. "Only one bed? Do we toss for it? I suppose I have to spend the night here, what's left of it, and slip back to my room about dawn looking suitably mussed and made-love-to. Oh, dear, and when I think of the way I sneaked around trying to keep people from knowing about Harold and me!" She laughed. "Well, it's going to be a refreshing change, being brazen about it. What happens afterward?"

I said, "In the morning, true love having blossomed during the wee hours, we head for Alabama on our way to Pensacola and home. Your home."

"Why Alabama?"

"There's no waiting period in Alabama. You just take a blood test and see the judge."

She looked quickly but didn't speak at once. Then she said, "I suppose that's still necessary."

"More than ever, I'd say. Now we have to see which one of them comes after you; and we've got to keep up the act for Mooney's sake, if not for Kroch's."

"Harold lives in Pensacola, don't forget. It will prove nothing if he follows us there."

"The roundabout way we'll drive, it'll prove something," I said. "Here are two things for you to keep in mind, Doc. One, like Orpheus and Eurydice, you don't look back." I grinned at her expression. "Don't act so surprised. It isn't polite. Us undercover types often read the classics to improve our minds when we're not dealing with murder and mayhem. Some of us do, anyway. Don't be an intellectual snob."

She flushed slightly. "I didn't mean… Well, maybe I did. Sorry."

"You don't look back," I went on. "I'll do the looking. You have no doubts, no suspicions. You're just a lady in love, bringing home a brand-new husband—one you married on the rebound, true, but that just makes you more determined to show people it's all perfectly lovely."

"Well, I'll try to look blissfully ignorant and… and inappropriately amorous." She hesitated. "You said two things. What's the other."

I reached down deliberately and gave a jerk to the hem of her skirt. "Number two," I said, "is, you keep your damn skirt down where it belongs."

It brought a gasp from her. It brought her upright in the chair. "*Really…!*"

I said, "I'm not an impressionable kid, but I'm not so damn ancient I don't react to normal stimuli, Doc. Now we both know you have attractive legs, nice nylons, and a pretty slip. We both know, too, that you're no longer quite the prim spinster lady you've been pretending to be. Well, whatever you learned from Mooney, please don't try it on me, doll. In public, we'll carry the lovey-dovey routine as far as necessary, but in private, like this, nix. You keep a reasonable amount of clothes on the body, and you keep them where they count." I stared at her in a hard way. "That is, of course, assuming that you *want* to keep it strictly business between us."

She was on her feet now, tugging her suit straight and buttoning her blouse with hands that weren't quite steady. "I'm sorry…!" Anger choked her briefly. "I'm very sorry if I've… disturbed you, Mr. Corcoran! It's late and I'm tired and just a bit tight; I didn't realize I was straining your self-control. It wasn't deliberate, I assure you!"

"Maybe it wasn't," I said. "And then again, maybe it

was. You don't look to me like a dame who shows a guy the view past the tops of her stockings without knowing it, drunk or sober. I don't quite follow the reasoning behind the tempting display, but it doesn't look like any gambit I read in the copy of Capablanca you so kindly lent me." I drew a long breath. "What I'm saying, Doc, is that if you want me to keep this love-and-marriage stuff on a business basis, you keep it that way, too. If you want to play, we'll play, and you'll find yourself flat on your back with your dress up and your girdle down so fast it'll make your head swim. Do I make myself perfectly clear?"

It was pretty crude; but the whole unbuttoned, inviting leggy bit had been too far out of character for me to let it pass unchallenged. A woman who, alone, would read about infinity fully dressed without a hair out of place wasn't going to lounge untidily and suggestively about a man's room without some purpose. The notion that came to mind was so crazy I had to check it out, even at the cost of being rude.

She stared at me for a moment, her eyes furious, her pale lips tightly compressed; then she laughed. It was a surprising laugh, for her, a real laugh, a woman's laugh… soft and throaty and triumphant.

"Corcoran," she murmured, "you're bluffing like hell!"

I looked at her sharply, and everything changed, as it does. It had been a long, complicated night, but everything was suddenly very plain and simple and I realized at last who—behind all the doubletalk and drinking and fancy acting—had actually been seducing whom.

"You're bluffing!" she breathed.

"Don't count on it," I said stiffly.

"You're bluffing!" she whispered. "You talk big but you won't… won't touch me. You don't dare!"

It had been a long time since I'd done anything because somebody dared me, but I'd already been strong-minded once that night, and I could see no good reason for it here. To be sure, Mac had warned me to be diplomatic, but under the circumstances it was a little hard to say where true diplomacy lay.

I reached out and took her glasses off for the second time that night. This time I really looked at her. The face was all right, once you started looking at it as the face of a woman instead of a genius and made allowance for the lack of lipstick. The eyes were fine without the glasses, a little bold but also, I was glad to see, a little scared, as if she didn't quite know what she was getting herself into besides a bed. Well, that made two of us.

I said, "The reception was poor at first, Doc, but now I read you loud and clear. Brief me. Do we lead up to the subject with a little breathless talk about love, or do we simply adjourn to the bed, approximately five feet away."

She licked her lips. "Let's not be hypocritical. You've probably gathered I've heard quite enough talk about love. I vote… I vote the meeting be adjourned as specified, before…" There was a shaky little pause… "before the lady loses her nerve!"

10

I woke up to hear her crying in the darkness beside me. I didn't ask why. Presumably she was crying in a general way for lost innocence and shattered illusions. It's a common complaint.

Presently she whispered, "Are you awake, Corcoran?"

"Yes."

"Did I wake you?"

"It doesn't matter."

"I'm sorry," she breathed. "I… it's just so cheap and dirty, that's all."

"Thanks," I said. "All testimonials gratefully accepted."

"I didn't mean you. I just meant, well, life in general."

"What you really meant was that for years you've been saving yourself for a great, sweet, tender passion like in the movies, and now you find yourself lying in a hotel bed in your underwear beside a strange man you don't particularly like."

She said, "Don't be sarcastic, damn you."

"Don't swear," I said. "I'll do the swearing around here. You're the intellectual type, remember?"

She laughed bitterly. "I don't feel very intellectual. I don't suppose I'd look very intellectual, either, if you could see me. The funny thing is, I don't think I even really know why I did it, why I badgered you into… well, into bed, damn it. And I'll swear all I want. To hell with you, Corcoran."

"For a girl who didn't know why she was doing it, you did it pretty well."

"I suppose I was really… I guess I was deliberately desecrating a shrine that had been sacred to a false god, if you know what I mean."

"Desecrating," I said. "Shrine. Such fancy words to use in bed at four in the morning… Ouch."

"What's the matter?"

"Your false god throws a mean punch. Do you feel like telling me? Just what did he do to bring the heavens crashing down?"

She started to speak sharply and checked herself. Then she was silent for a little. At last she laughed in the darkness and said, "You're being sarcastic again, but your description is pretty accurate, unfortunately. But when a woman is fool enough to wait until thirty to learn about sex and love, I guess she's asking for a major catastrophe. It was like a dream at first. I'd never experienced anything like it. I'd never experienced much of anything along those lines. He brought me flowers. He bought me little presents—perfume, stockings, lingerie. He… he made me feel like a woman, Corcoran. He even made me feel like a beautiful woman. It had never happened to me before."

Her frankness was a little embarrassing, even in the dark. I said, "Buy yourself a lipstick and it could happen again. You're not really nauseating, you know."

"Thanks," she murmured. "Thanks for the charming compliment, charmingly phrased. I'll treasure it always."

"No charge," I said. "Let's get to the point where he lowered the boom."

"It was a Friday, I think," she said. "Yes, I'm sure it was a Friday, the end of the week, at ten in the morning. I had an appointment. I was still seeing him, well, professionally too. They were laughing," she said in a flat voice.

"Who was laughing?"

"I came into the office a little early. I really wanted to be late to show him… Well, I just wanted to stroll in casually a few minutes late. You know, so it wouldn't look as if seeing him was very important in my life. But when I got out of the elevator it was still a few minutes early. I just couldn't help myself. I'd seen him the night before but I still couldn't help myself. You know how it is."

"Sure," I said. "I know how it is. I guess."

"The reception room was empty. I started back there and heard them. They were talking about me in the examining room, Harold and the nurse, or receptionist, an obvious, well-developed little blonde in one of those white nylon uniforms, you know the kind I mean, the kind that are practically transparent, worn over something pink, always. Miss Darden was the way I knew her, the way he'd always referred to her, but now he was calling her Dottie. The way they were talking made the relationship between them absolutely clear. They'd come to an understanding long ago. You know. She was so sure of herself and of him that she wasn't even jealous; his extracurricular activities merely amused her. Do I have to tell you exactly what they said about me? What he said?"

"No," I said, "but in fairness you've got to remember that there aren't many things a man can say to one woman he's sleeping with when discussing another. He's practically got to make it sound as if the only reason he has anything to do with the second dame is for money, influence, or laughs."

"Laughs!" she breathed. "How did you know? It was a hilarious joke they shared. I was. Something to titter about together while waiting for me to arrive so they could greet me looking very sober and professional. I want to vomit when I think of it, Corcoran. I was such an idiot about him. It was as if I'd been hypnotized to do mad things and couldn't help myself... And then to hear them *laughing*! I wanted to kill myself."

"Instead of which," I said, "you marched right down and said you'd take the crazy assignment you'd refused earlier. The idea of having the U.S. government arrange a whirlwind love affair for you, and provide a husband you could get rid of after he'd served your purpose, suddenly looked real good. It was a way of telling Dr. Harold Mooney he hadn't hurt you a bit; it was a way of showing him he wasn't the only bird in the bush."

"Yes," she said. "Yes, of course."

"My chief kind of wondered what made you change your mind," I said. "I wondered myself, a bit. You didn't look like somebody who'd take on a job like this just for kicks. Well, now you'd better get out of here before the place wakes up."

I switched on the light and looked at her. She sat up and hastily pulled up a strap of the pretty slip she'd retained while shedding the rest of her clothes—a present from Mooney, the romantic flowers-and-lingerie dispenser, I guessed, now. I wondered if it had given her some kind of perverse satisfaction to wear his intimate gift to bed with another man. Her bare shoulders were square and strong-looking, but smooth and white.

"Well, you don't have to stare!" she protested, blushing.

I grinned. "Now she gets modest," I said. "*Now* what are you doing?"

"My hair—"

"What do you want to do, spoil the effect after we've gone to all this trouble to make it authentic?"

She glanced at me quickly. After a moment she smiled. "Oh, is that what we were doing? I didn't know."

I said, "Well, you don't want to look as if you'd been doing research in the Library of Congress, Doc. If Handsome Harold is lurking outside, you want to confirm his darkest suspicions, don't you? Just pull on your skirt and blouse, stick your feet into your shoes, make a bundle of everything else, and dash for the stairs. Call me the minute you reach your room, so I'll know you're okay. The coffee shop opens at six. I'll meet you there for breakfast."

A minute or so later she was standing at the door rather uncertainly, hesitating to show herself outside like that, disheveled and not completely dressed. The funny thing was, she looked kind of young and pretty with her severe hairdo tumbling about her face and the color of embarrassment in her cheeks.

"Corcoran?"

"Yes?"

"I want you to know it wasn't premeditated. I had every intention of keeping you at a very proper distance. Please believe me."

"Sure," I said.

If she wanted to lie for the sake of her self-respect, I wasn't going to argue; and maybe she'd just happened to be wearing pretty stuff under the tweed tonight, even though it did seem like kind of a coincidence.

"It was seeing him and hearing him trying to tell me about misunderstandings in that smooth, patronizing way. I just had to do something to erase, well, certain memories. I hope you're not disgusted or... or offended."

"Offended?" I said. "Don't be silly, Doc. It beats the hell out of chess."

She looked startled and fled. Two minutes later the phone rang; she'd made it safely. I acknowledged her report and lay for a little while looking at the ceiling, while daylight stole into the room. She wasn't the only one with memories to erase. At last I grimaced at my thoughts and got up to shave. I had half my face lathered when the phone rang. I went back into the bedroom and picked it up.

"You're up early, friend," said the voice of the local man who'd given me instructions before, the one I'd never seen. "Or were you up?"

"Do you care?"

"If I'm not allowed to sleep, why should anyone else be? I'm supposed to transmit a report on a Harold Mooney, M.D. Nothing."

"Nothing?"

"Well, nothing significant. Bachelor's, Hopkins. M.D., Hopkins. Internship, Chicago. Private practice, Pensacola since fifty-nine. Doing all right financially. Well, he should be. Apparently he's got the bedside looks and manner, and he's no worse a butcher than anybody else, I guess. But he's clean as new-fallen snow. At least on a preliminary check. They're still digging." There was a little pause. "That's as far as security is concerned. We're not interested in his morals. Or are we?"

"We might be."

"There are indications he's something of an all-around medical charm boy, or just very, very susceptible. His office nurses aren't picked entirely for their academic records, let's say, and there's a high turnover. And there have been whispers about the doctor-patient relationship in certain instances. Just whispers."

"I see," I said. "But there's no chance of his being offbeat in other ways, say politically? No chance of anybody's having got to him?"

"You supply the crystal ball, I'll read it," said the voice on the phone. "Chance? Sure there's a chance. There's always a chance. They may come up with something on thorough investigation. But this guy's just interested in money and women as far as I can see; he's not the kind to go haywire politically. And the material looks unpromising if you're hunting a potential killer."

I said, "After you've cut up enough dead bodies in medical school, I shouldn't think a live one would bother you much. And doctors have access to very convenient drugs, and ways of covering things up that aren't available to the layman. The man we're looking for doesn't necessarily have to be a pineapple and tommy-gun artist, you know."

"Still, there's better homicidal stuff around," the voice said.

"Kroch?"

"They finally found him for you. You were right, he's a pro alright, but they were checking the wrong lists. They were looking for someone Grandpa Taussig would be likely to recruit, someone from the regular herd, close at hand. This one is a stray from another ranch entirely."

I said, "Meaning what?"

"Hold onto your hat," said the voice on the phone. "Kroch used to be one of Reinhard Heydrich's Nazi strongarm boys. An angry young man with a club, but his specialty was the pistol. He went in for small calibers, quiet and precise. Not what you'd expect from the crude physical characteristics, is it? Heydrich had great faith in young Kroch, it says here, and used him frequently. After the British elimination team got the Hangman, Kroch disappeared. Yours is the first report on him since the war. It was thought he was dead."

"Well, he isn't," I said. "So he's an ex-Gestapo bully-boy. Those former Nazis keep cropping up all over these days, don't they? I had to go down into Mexico after one just last summer, a gent named Von Sachs who was going to establish a Fourth Reich over here, or something. He was a regulation sonofabitch, fascist style, but he handled a machete real pretty for a while." I frowned. "Any theories on how Kroch comes to be working for the Communists, if he really is?"

"It's not unusual. A lot of those lads didn't care who they swung a blackjack for as long as they were paid. And Taussig would be needing a lot of manpower for a scheme as ambitious as this one. A trained goon like Kroch could set his own price, almost. Washington likes Kroch better than Mooney, friend. They want you to put the show on the road as soon as possible. If Kroch follows and the other one doesn't, nab him."

"Sure," I said. "And what if they both follow? Or neither does?"

"Don't borrow trouble. Start driving and use the mirror first. See what comes along behind. But watch yourself. This boy's no rabbit; it'll take more than a figure-four trap to catch and hold him."

"It'll take more than a harsh word to make him talk, too," I said.

"That's not your worry unless you want it to be. You present the body, breathing, and experts will take it from there. They'll get it out of him. Any more questions?"

I hesitated. "One. Antoinette Vail. Is she being watched?"

"She's covered. She hasn't shown yet this morning. Why?"

"No reason," I said.

I didn't really know why I'd asked the question. Toni didn't belong in the case, except that I'd dragged her in for a diversion. Nobody would thank me for being concerned about a kid who was just an irrelevant nuisance, not even the kid herself.

11

The coffee shop had a white tiled floor and old-fashioned-looking tables and chairs, but no booths or jukebox. I seated Olivia at a corner table, acting as if we'd just happened to meet in the doorway by accident.

She was wearing a dress this morning, I noticed. It wasn't much to cheer about; one of the fashionably loose, baggy, blousy jobs that look very smart on a model built like a broomstick, which she wasn't. It was some kind of brownish jersey. They tell me that knitted stuff is very practical for traveling. I'm glad to hear it's good for something. Decoration-wise, it always looks like a variation of burlap to me.

Still, it was a dress and it wasn't tweed. There were other changes.

"For God's sake," I said.

"What is it... Oh."

She blushed a little and looked self-conscious. It was pink and innocuous, but it was real lipstick. Pretty soon she'd break down and powder her nose and everything. It gave me a funny feeling. I mean, after all, it was just a job for me. I didn't really want the responsibility of guiding the woman to a new view of life.

I'd had enough of personal feelings on this job. I could still hear Antoinette's voice: *Why, I really liked you! And you set me up for this!* Dr. Olivia Mariassy was just another decoy, I reminded myself firmly. Unlike Toni, she knew she was being used, but God only knew what I'd have to set her up for in the end.

"It isn't nice to stare," she said. "It isn't nice to make fun of me."

"Who's making fun?"

"I thought a bride-to-be would naturally pretty herself up a little," she said defensively. "We're still getting married today, aren't we? Wasn't that the plan?"

"That's still the plan," I said. "In fact we've got orders from Washington to put it into execution as soon as possible. They want us to separate the sheep from the goats, or the sheep from the goat, singular. Whichever of the two follows, we're supposed to take him and turn him over to the wrecking crew pronto."

She glanced at me quickly. "The wrecking crew?"

"The I-team," I said. "The interrogation team. The experts. That is, unless we want to ask the questions ourselves."

She shivered slightly. "It isn't very nice, is it?"

"Not very."

"I wish there were some other way. I don't think it'll

be a nice thing to remember, that I was a party to it and helped lure him into the trap. Whichever one of them it is. No matter if his job is to kill me, it won't be pleasant. Is this man Taussig really so important? What's he like?"

"I've never met him socially," I said. "I gather, if you met him on the street, you might think you were looking at Albert Einstein. Well, Emil is kind of a genius, too, in his own field. As for his importance, that's not a question you're supposed to ask, Doc. What do you want, a long patriotic speech about how the lives of innocent people and the fate of nations all depend on somebody's getting to Taussig in time?"

She sighed. "I know, some things you just have to accept. I'm not always happy about the uses to which science is being put these days, but I don't stop my research for that reason." She paused and said in the same tone of voice, "Talking about sheep—"

"What?"

"Talking about sheep and goats, we have company, Mr. Corcoran." She was looking beyond me. She leaned forward and covered my hand with hers. "Paul," she said, "darling—"

I got the idea. "Sweetheart!" I said, looking into her eyes with adoration.

Then Mooney was standing there with his horn-rims and heavy tweeds, looking as if he hadn't had much sleep. Despite his haggardness, I noticed, he was smoothly shaved. I caught a whiff of some masculine-smelling lotion as I got to my feet. He raised his hand quickly.

"Please! I'm not... I just came to apologize. I just wasn't myself last night."

I said aggressively, "Whoever you were, that guy's got a couple of punches coming."

Olivia was still holding my hand. She pulled me back. "Please, darling. It's such a lovely morning, let's not spoil it. If Harold wants to apologize, why don't you let him?" Her voice was smooth. She smiled at Mooney. "Go on, Harold. Apologize. Tell Paul you're sorry you hit him when he wasn't looking."

I said, "He'd be a damn sight sorrier if he'd hit me when I *was* looking!"

"Paul! You're not being nice. Please, darling... Go on, Harold."

She smiled at him sweetly until he mumbled something; then she made us shake hands like two quarrelsome boys. Finally she asked him to pull up a chair and join us. It wasn't the most pleasant breakfast I've ever eaten, but she enjoyed it thoroughly. She had a fine time making him squirm. It was a side of her character I hadn't seen before, and it made me feel better. A girl with that much acid in her system wasn't going to be hurt as easily as I'd feared.

Finally she pushed back her chair and patted my hand. "You finish your coffee, darling. I'm going upstairs to pack." She turned to Harold. "Why don't you come up and watch me, Harold. There's something I want to tell you."

I watched them rise together. Being just a slob of a Denver reporter, I didn't get up. "I'll be along as soon as I've finished," I said.

She leaned over and kissed me on the mouth, "Don't hurry," she said, laughing, "and don't be jealous, darling. I'm perfectly safe with Harold, aren't I, Harold?"

Harold didn't answer. He was taking in the kiss and the endearments. He'd already spotted the unaccustomed lipstick and the way she couldn't seem to keep her hands off me, and he was obviously wishing he'd taken the opportunity to jump up and down on me with both feet last night. Whether he was truly jealous, or whether I was interfering with plans that had nothing to do with love, remained to be seen.

I watched them leave together. Olivia was prattling away happily, making him wait for the big news until they were alone. She obviously had no doubt about the nature of his feelings, and she was getting a big kick out of being able to announce her forthcoming marriage to him and tell him that he really hadn't hurt her a bit. Quite the contrary, he'd helped her, like the ugly duckling, to discover her true, swanlike self in marriage to a fine man like me.

Well, she had it coming. It was her payment for helping us. She'd probably earn every happy, sadistic moment of it before she was through. But it was also revealing, and I couldn't help thinking wryly that Olivia Mariassy was turning out rather different from the cool, detached, scientific personality with whom I'd been expecting to work.

The waitress refilled my coffee cup, but it just wasn't my morning to finish anything, shaving or eating, for that damn instrument invented by Alex G. Bell. I'd just taken a couple of sips when a phone buzzed in the corner. The girl who answered it looked around, spotted me sitting there alone, and came over.

"Are you Mr. Corcoran? You're wanted on the house phone."

I went over fast, but not fast enough to keep from realizing that I'd slipped badly. Daylight and Kroch's continued absence had made me careless, and I'd let Olivia go upstairs without protection, unless you wanted to count Mooney, who might be just the opposite.

"Yes?" I said into the mouthpiece. "Corcoran here."

"Paul?" It was Olivia's voice, but very different from the gay, bright, malicious tone she'd been using when last heard. "Paul, come up to my room right away, please!"

"Sure."

I took the stairs rather than wait for the elevator. I had the little knife in my hand as I approached the door. It's not a switch-blade, but there are ways of opening it fast, one-handed, just the same. I knocked on the door and went through it fast and hard when it started to open.

I could have saved myself the melodrama. There were only two people inside, Olivia and Mooney. She was the one who'd let me in. There was blood on her hands. He was lying on the bed with his coat off and his shirt-sleeve ripped away. His face was gray. There was a hotel towel under his bare arm to catch the blood that dripped from a bullet-hole in his biceps.

12

Olivia closed the door gingerly, leaving smears on the knob nevertheless.

I said, "So he's a heel. You didn't have to shoot him." She glanced at me irritably. "Don't be silly. Where would I get a gun?"

I could have told her. She hadn't been far from the one I carry in my suitcase on several occasions during the night. But even supposing she could have swiped it for purposes of vengeance or something, one blast from that sawed-off regulation cannon would have aroused the whole hotel. It also would have nearly torn Mooney's arm off. He'd obviously been shot with something considerably smaller and quieter than a .38 Special. I remembered that there was a man around who specialized in small-caliber weapons, according to the report I'd just received that morning.

"Olivia...!" That was Mooney's voice, weak and panicky.

"It's all right, Harold. You're not really losing much

blood. Let it wash itself out." She turned to me. "Help me off with my dress, please. Be careful, my hands are kind of messy. I don't want to get blood all over it." She waited while I unfastened the belt and zipper and worked the dress down her arms and, cautiously, over her hands; then she stepped out of it while I held it low. "Hang it over that chair and get my bag out of the closet, a brown leather bag," she said.

I glanced toward Mooney. "Hadn't he better have a tourniquet or something?"

She said, "Get the bag, Paul. Leave the practice of medicine to me, please."

"Sure."

She was in charge, there was no doubt about it. There was no seductive lingerie today, just a white slip without frills. Although a little bare on top, it could have been a surgeon's gown the unself-conscious way she wore it. By the time I'd got the bag, she was sitting on the edge of the bed, examining the wound. Mooney gasped with pain and she shook her head irritably.

"Don't be such a baby, Harold." She glanced at me as I came up. "Just put it down there and open it. Then follow my directions carefully…"

"Wait a minute!" I said, remembering that, as far as Mooney was concerned, I was supposed to be a reasonably law-abiding character, as least where serious matters like gunshot wounds were concerned. "Wait a minute. I don't know what the hell happened in here, but hadn't we better call the police?"

"It was a man," Mooney whispered. "A big, bald man with protruding ears. I'd recognize him anywhere. He was hiding in the bathroom. I told him… I protested…"

Olivia said, with a meaningful glance at me, "That's right, Paul. It was a prowler. I haven't had time to see if anything is missing, and I haven't anything worth stealing anyway. I can't imagine what he was doing here, maybe just working from room to room."

Her voice was cool and matter of fact. She was pretty damn good, I had to admit. She might have been clumsy yesterday evening but she was catching on fast.

I said in my innocent role, "Sure, but what about the cops? They like to be notified in cases like this. It's a notion they have."

She looked at the man on the bed. Her voice was tart. "I don't really think Harold wants the folks back in Pensacola to read in the papers that he was shot in my hotel room in New Orleans, no matter how innocently he happened to be there."

Mooney shook his head quickly. "No. Please. If we can avoid publicity—"

"I'm quite capable of fixing up a little bullet-hole," Olivia said. "Now please open my bag, Paul, and get the bottle of peroxide, hydrogen peroxide, and the applicators… Oh, and twist up a towel or something for Harold to bite on when he feels like screaming, will you? We're going to have to do this without anesthesia, and Harold is rather sensitive about pain, aren't you, Harold? I mean, his own pain, of course."

Her face was expressionless, but the peroxide bubbled viciously as it hit the raw flesh of the wound. Actually it doesn't really sting, not like iodine or Merthiolate, but watching it you'd think you were being consumed alive. Mooney started by watching the proceedings bravely enough, but he quickly turned his face away, looking sick.

"So much for the preliminaries," Olivia said calmly. "Now we're going to have to go in and clean it thoroughly. Fortunately the bullet went clear through, but it may have carried along dirt or scraps of cloth… All right, Paul."

She made a sharp little gesture. I was in position; I had the twisted towel in both hands, like a garrote. I got it between his teeth as he opened his mouth to yell, and I held it there. It wasn't the first time I'd helped patch up a guy when silence was necessary. Presently he fainted, which was nice for everybody.

"There," Olivia said at last, completing a neat white dressing that covered both entry and exit holes. She grimaced. "I look as if I'd been sticking pigs, don't I?" Her voice was light.

I said, "Cut it out. You don't have to impress me, and he's out cold. I don't like working with screwballs, Doc. Don't let this vengeance kick get out of hand."

She looked at me across the bed. "What do you mean?" she asked innocently.

"What's this about not having any anesthetic? I bet you could have squirted something into him to make it easier if you'd wanted to."

She turned away and went to the bathroom door and

looked back. "Why should I want to make it easy for him, my dear?" she asked quietly. "Bring him to and get him out of here. He's doctor enough to know how to treat it while it heals, I hope. Tell him I hope he has the decency not to try to see me or speak to me again. Not that decency is a word I'd normally associate with him!"

She went into the bathroom and pulled the door closed behind her.

I cleaned up around the place, wiping the phone and doorknob where she'd left traces, and making a bundle of the stained towels. They presented no problem. Everybody swipes hotel towels. Finally I took a careful look around and saw where the bullet had ended up in the plaster wall after passing through Mooney's arm. I dug it out with my knife, fingered it—a .22—and dropped it into my pocket. By the time I was through, the patient was beginning to stir uneasily. I went over to him. He opened his eyes to look at me.

"She says you'll live, much to her regret," I said. "Let's get your jacket on and I'll see you to your room. But first I'd like a run-down on what happened. You say there was a man in the bathroom?"

Mooney licked his lips. "Yes. Olivia went in there for her toothbrush or something. I heard her gasp; then she was backing out stiffly as if she'd just missed stepping on a snake. This man followed her in. He had a little tiny pistol. It looked like a toy. He had tremendous hands."

"Go on," I said.

"He was a big man," Mooney said. "He made us stand

against the wall over there. He looked at me and asked who the hell I was. He seemed very annoyed with me for being there. I told him my name and I told him… well, I protested against his manner. He was really very rude and overbearing. I told him…" He stopped.

I looked at the man on the bed wearily. He still smelled of that virile, masculine shaving lotion. Nowadays we men are supposed to smell pretty, too. I remembered a number of good men I'd known who'd generally smelled of sweat or horses or fast-car lubricants, sometimes of smokeless powder or that acrid variation the British call cordite. I felt old and tired.

"I know," I said gently. "Oh, I know. You told him he couldn't get away with it."

Mooney looked startled. "Why, yes! How did you know?"

"Because that's how damn fools always get themselves shot, trying to sound brave at the point of a gun," I said. "If you'd kept your trap shut, you probably wouldn't have got hurt. They ought to have a high-school course in not talking back to a man with a gun. It might save more lives than driving lessons."

"I couldn't believe he'd be crazy enough to really shoot!" Mooney protested. "I mean, it was so pointless. What did it gain him?"

I said, "Well, for one thing, it shut you up, didn't it?" Kroch had obviously been on edge. Listening to the pompous grandstanding of an amateur hero had been too much. Well, it showed that the opposition was subject to nerves and irritability like anybody else; it also showed he didn't kid around much. But it didn't explain his motive for being there. Obviously Mooney's presence had surprised and annoyed him. The question was, had he been waiting for Olivia, hoping to catch her alone, or had he hoped to catch me, too?

I picked up Mooney's jacket. The holes were almost invisible in the thick tweed, and what blood there was, was on the inside.

"On your feet," I said. "Let's get this on you so you look respectable. Our prowler friend didn't happen to indicate what he was looking for in here, did he?"

"No. No, he didn't give any intimation… Ahh, that hurts!"

I had to steady him and work the jacket on gently; then, when we reached his room, I had to help him off with it again. I looked at him sitting on the edge of the hotel bed, pale and sick in his stained, half-sleeveless shirt, and I knew I'd been wrong about him. He wasn't our man.

I don't mean we're all heroes; I don't mean we're all iron men. But he wasn't acting and he hadn't been acting—he wasn't that good; and they use a little harder material for agents than Dr. Harold Mooney had displayed this morning. This wasn't a man you'd send out to run the terrible risks involved in committing murder on signal. Olivia had been right. He was just a handsome phony.

I said, "Olivia says she doesn't want to see or hear from you again. We're getting married, you know."

"Yes." He licked his lips. "Yes, she told me. Just before that man—"

"In case you're wondering," I said, "in case you have the remotest little idea resembling, shall we say, blackmail or anything like that, I'd better tell you that I know all about it, you and her. There's nothing you can threaten her with, because she's already told me everything. I know I'm getting something pretty good, and I know I'm getting it on the rebound, and I don't give a damn…"

Well, you can complete the parting speech for yourself. I was the sterling character willing to forgive the poor girl one mistake; I was also the dissipated rounder reformed by a woman's love. Maybe it was inconsistent but it sounded swell. We parted on a very high plane indeed. When I got back to Olivia's room, she was scrubbed and dressed and her bags were packed.

"How is he?" she asked.

I said, "I'm sorry I kept you waiting, but it took a little time to find the pliers."

She frowned quickly. "Pliers?"

"Sure," I said. "To pull out his fingernails and toenails by the roots. Wasn't that what you wanted? I had the iron heating while I did it so I wouldn't waste any time burning out his eyes afterwards—"

"Damn you," she said. "What are you talking about? I didn't hurt him deliberately. Well, not much." I didn't say anything. She looked down. "Paul," she whispered.

"Yes, Doc?"

"I still love him. You know that, don't you?"

"Sure," I said, "but the way you show it, I hope to hell I can keep you hating me. Come on, we've got a date to get married, remember?"

13

We got the job done in a small town in Alabama, the name doesn't matter. It wasn't the fanciest wedding I'd ever had. I went the cutaway-and-white-satin route once. To be strictly accurate, it was right after the war and I was in uniform—the first time I'd worn my soldier suit in almost four years. What I'd really been doing overseas in various other costumes was an official secret, not to be revealed to anybody, not even my bride.

I was making like an Army officer on terminal leave, therefore, but some of the other male participants wore those streamlined tailcoats, and the bridesmaids were in tulle, if I've got the name right. It was very formal and pretty, and everybody said the bride looked perfectly lovely, but it didn't take. She learned a little too much about me eventually, and didn't like what she learned; and now she's married to a rancher in Nevada and the kids are growing up on horseback and calling him daddy. I guess he's better daddy material than I am, at that.

Olivia and I had lunch in the town afterward so anybody who wanted to check on the ceremony would have time to do so. The meal was a silent one. I suppose we both felt awkward about our new legal relationship. Finished, we got back into the car.

It was hers, a little foreign job with the engine behind. I guess she'd felt Volkswagens were getting too commonplace with the intellectual crowd; she'd got herself a French Renault, plain black with gray vinyl upholstery and all of thirty-two horsepower working through a three-speed shift, which isn't enough gears to get real efficiency out of so small a mill. I got behind the wheel, started the machinery stirring in back and drove away, watching the mirror.

It was a waste of time. Nothing showed but the ordinary southern small-town traffic. Nothing followed us away from there except a Ford pickup with Alabama plates, which turned off onto a dirt road after a couple of miles.

"It still looks like a water haul," I reported at last.

"What?"

"A country colloquialism, Mrs. Corcoran," I said. "That's what you say when you've come a long way for very little. Not that I'm running down the holy state of matrimony, you understand."

She smiled, and stopped smiling, and looked thoughtful. "Could Kroch just be giving us rope, so to speak, counting on picking us up in Pensacola?"

"Why should he think I'd take you home to Pensacola where your friends and colleagues are? As of this morning, he had no reason to believe my intentions were honorable. Having softened up the lady, wouldn't I be much more likely to take her to a lonely love nest by the seashore?" I shook my head ruefully. "If he's our man, he ought to be sticking with you. If he doesn't show, we've figured wrong somewhere."

"But if he isn't our man, why was he hiding in my room?" Olivia protested. "It doesn't make sense.

"If he is our man, why was he hiding in your room?" I countered. "Mr. Kroch seems to have a habit of not making much sense. I have a hunch, the kind you get in this business, that he was waiting there to kill me."

She looked startled. "That's kind of farfetched, isn't it? Why would he want to kill you? And why would he think you'd come here?"

I said, "After the cozy way you'd spent the night in my room, it wasn't too unlikely that I'd visit yours. If you came alone, you could be made to call me. I should have anticipated something of the sort, but I'd seen no indications that the guy was around and I'm having kind of a hard time following his mental processes. But he was annoyed with Mooney for being there, wasn't he? Presumably he'd expected somebody else, me. As for his motive, he's already served notice that he doesn't like interference."

She said, "It was my room, after all. The most likely possibility is that he was just waiting for me."

I said, "The answer to that is that you're sitting beside me very much alive, thank God. If he'd wanted you, if the word had come through that it was time for him to act, he'd have got you. What was there to stop him, with your efficient bodyguard slurping coffee three stories below?" I made a wry face at the windshield. "He had you, but he didn't kill you. He just shot Mooney in the arm and took off... Wait a minute! We're overlooking something. Suppose he was waiting for just the man he got. Suppose he was waiting for Dr. Harold Mooney."

She was staring at me. "You can't think there's anything between Harold and Kroch!"

"I'm trying out the idea. It has possibilities."

"It's absolutely insane!" she protested. "I should think you'd be satisfied about Harold after this morning. We agreed he's not the stuff one makes secret agents out of."

I said, "Sure. He couldn't be trusted to do the work alone. I'll grant that. But that doesn't mean he isn't the stuff one makes secret agents' accomplices out of. Suppose Kroch is our man after all, but suppose he's playing it real cagey. He hasn't shown previously, has he? You'd never seen his face before, to remember it?"

"No, but—"

"It's a face you wouldn't forget if you saw it twice, even just passing it on the street," I said. "And don't think Kroch doesn't know it. It's his handicap in this business, as my height is mine. He'll be forever figuring ways to get around it. Well, suppose he's using Mooney as his eyes, and keeping his ugly, conspicuous self under cover. Mooney isn't scheduled for any heavy work. Anybody can see he isn't up to it. He just keeps track of you, acting the romantic lover. That's why he followed you here in a panic, not because he was scared of a scandal, but because he couldn't afford to lose contact with you or Kroch would have his hide. His job is to keep you located in a general sort of way. When the time comes, Kroch moves in and makes the kill."

Olivia winced. I guess it wasn't a pleasant idea to have tossed at you casually.

Then she said impatiently, "That's ridiculous! Harold has no interest whatever in politics. Why would he—"

"Does Harold lead such a blameless life that you can't imagine anybody blackmailing him, Doc? Is he such a strong character he'd tell a blackmailer to publish and be damned?"

She was silent for a moment, then she said quickly: "But Kroch shot him! Doesn't that prove—"

"In the arm?" I said. "A neat, small-caliber flesh wound with a doctor available—two doctors if you count Mooney himself—if anything went wrong, like a severed artery? It's been done before by people with complicated motives and mentalities. Why did Mooney come around this morning to apologize? He's hardly the apologetic type. If you hadn't invited him to your room, maybe he'd have invited himself on some pretext."

"To get shot? Harold would never agree to that. You saw the way he reacted."

"He didn't have to know what was going to happen. He could just have had orders to make an appearance there with you at a certain time. Kroch's acting surprised and annoyed by his presence could have been just a cover-up. And after the shooting, Mooney didn't dare squawk." I drew a long breath. "Look, Kroch knows I have him spotted. He can guess I'm also suspicious of Harold, the way he's been hanging around you. This could be Kroch's way of whitewashing Harold and taking all the suspicion on himself. That would leave the handsome doctor, pale and romantic-looking, with his arm in a sling, free to keep up the surveillance unsuspected. Meanwhile Kroch crawls back into his hole, wherever it is, gets regular reports on you from Mooney, cleans his little popgun, and waits for Der Tag."

Olivia shook her head. "I don't believe it!" There was a little pause. She gave a short laugh. "I guess I just don't want to believe it, Paul. It was bad enough thinking Harold at least found me… well, attractive enough at the start. If he did the whole thing under orders, that doesn't leave me any pride at all."

I said, "It could be that Kroch found the situation between you and Mooney already established when he came on the job, and simply looked around for a way to take advantage of it."

"It's a nice thought," she said wryly. "It makes everything much better. Now all I have to face is the fact that Harold is willing to help another man murder me to save his own skin…"

The little car buzzed on down the black highway between the trees of one of those dry-looking southern pine forests. When you come from the West, as I do, you're apt to think everything east of the Mississippi is built up solidly like suburban New York, but it isn't true. There are still some good big forests there, and some bleak lonely island beaches that haven't yet been turned into replicas of Coney Island.

I had one of those offshore strips of white sand near Pensacola in mind as I drove. I'd seen it from the air, returning from the carrier with Lt. (jg) Braithwaite, and I'd talked it over with Olivia, who'd been out there in the summer. She'd agreed that at this time of year, too cold for swimming or picnicking, you could commit murder at leisure there, or any other crime you happened to have in mind. The difficulty would come in getting our subject out there, particularly if he was using another man as a front.

I noticed that Olivia was twisting her new wedding ring on her finger. "It's a funny feeling," she said.

"What is?"

"Being married. Like this. In cold blood, so to speak. Paul?"

"Yes?"

She didn't look at me. "Please remember that in spite of last night it's purely a business proposition."

I said, rather stiffly, "If you mean I'm not to presume on the wedding license—"

"No, that's not what I mean," she said quickly. "But it's not as if we were in love with each other or trusted each other, really. It's not as if we really knew each other and expected to spend a lifetime together."

"What are you trying to say, Doc?"

She didn't look up. "Just that I'm not really a very nice person. I used to think I was. Nicey-nice. Prissy, even. A very high-minded and moral citizen. But I'm just not, that's all. The last few days—the last few weeks— have shown me things about myself that are rather frightening. But you're not marrying me for my character or personality, or my looks or money or background, or anything like that, are you? You picked me out for this job, or your chief did. It wasn't my idea. Please remember that. So if you should learn something about me one day, something not very pleasant, you'll have no right to complain that I tricked or deceived you. Will you?"

I said, "Is this another of those little personal matters you don't care to discuss, Doc? The last one got me a sock on the jaw, as I recall. I hope you don't have any more pugilistic boy friends hanging around."

"No," she said. "No, it's nothing like that. It's just… No, I can't say any more. It's not my secret."

I looked at her for a moment longer, looked ahead, and straightened the little car out at the edge of the pavement. For some reason I found myself remembering that Mariassy was a Hungarian name, and that Emil Taussig had once pulled a big, murderous job in Budapest, or tried. It would be a hell of a coincidence if there was any connection, and if there was one, I couldn't think what it would be, but it made me uneasy just the same.

"You pick the damndest times to go into your mystery-woman act," I said irritably. "The secret life of Olivia Mariassy. Nuts!"

"I shouldn't have said anything. I was just trying to keep the record straight, for my conscience's sake. It's really completely irrelevant."

"Sure," I said. "So was Mooney, you said. If it's not your secret, whose is it?" I looked at her again. She shook her head minutely; she wasn't telling. I said, "Doc, if you'd heard that darling-never-trust-me line as often as I have—"

"And always from a beautiful female agent, I suppose." Olivia's voice was dry. "And usually in bed, no doubt. It must be a fascinating life."

"You'll have an opportunity to judge it for yourself in just a moment," I said. "I'm going to give it a try while we're still on the road. If somebody's tailing us, they're very good, and they're obviously not going to give us a look at them driving. I think we'd better disappear from the highway temporarily. Get the guy worrying about losing us, if there is a guy, and maybe he'll show himself while we lie in the woods, watching. He may even come in after us, if we arrange it right."

She looked at me, and touched her tongue to her lips. "And if he does?"

"If he does," I said, "we've got orders to take him."

"You mean right now? Right here? I thought you said you were going to wait and lure him out to one of the beaches—"

"We'll keep the beaches in reserve," I said. "This piney country looks pretty good. I'm pretty good in the woods, if I do say so myself."

Olivia shivered slightly. "All right," she breathed. "All right. You don't mind if I'm a little frightened, do you? But it will be nice to have it over, if it works. If there is someone." She hesitated. "You'll have to tell me what to do."

I told her.

14

The road I picked to turn off on was just two ruts among the trees. It ran straight back into a patch of timber that promised adequate cover. I drove off the highway a reasonable distance but not so far that the Renault couldn't be spotted by someone with sharp eyes driving by.

Stopping, I took Olivia into my arms. It was supposed to look very passionate from a distance—after all, we'd just got married, and a little private clinch was in order—but the French, for all their sexy reputation, must not go in for that stuff much or they wouldn't put the handbrake and gearshift lever where they do.

Still, it wasn't exactly a mechanical performance. I mean, we were both human and we'd spent some time in the same bed the night before. She still knew where the noses went. I was aware of traffic on the highway, but I won't claim I kept an accurate count of every car that went past. We were both a bit breathless when the time came to break.

"One of these days," I said, releasing her, "one of these days we'll have to do that just for fun, Doc. Scene Two coming up. Do you have a blanket on board?"

"Blanket?" She had her hands to her hair. She wasn't looking at me. There was color in her cheeks and she looked just like a woman who'd been kissed and not at all like a scientific institution. "No, I'm afraid there's no blanket. Why?"

"Don't be innocent," I said. "Because of what would follow naturally between two newlyweds in a secluded spot like this, that's why. Because of what obviously can't be done in a car this size by a man my size. Well, my topcoat will have to do. Leave your damn hair alone and come on."

I grabbed the coat from the rear seat, got out, and joined her on the other side of the car, putting my arm around her to make it look good if somebody was watching. A vehicle went past on the highway doing at least eighty; that one wasn't looking out for anything but cops. I led her toward a patch of brush that offered privacy. Inside there was enough space at the foot of a big pine to spread my coat. Olivia sat down and checked her stockings for snags, then looked up smiling.

"I'm not supposed to be thinking of my appearance, am I?"

Her voice was cool and steady now, and I found myself wondering if that was really what she'd been thinking. *It wasn't my idea,* she'd said. *You'll have no right to complain that I tricked or deceived you.* It was as clear a warning as I could expect.

It was a hell of a case, I reflected. Nobody was really acting right, not Kroch, not the woman who was supposed to be my partner in the assignment, the woman who was now, according to law, my wife. Even Mooney, the lightweight, couldn't seem to stay in character either as a sincere lover or a panicky seducer or a cowardly accomplice. And in some respects I wasn't being very consistent myself, although I preferred not to examine that idea too closely.

I said, business-like: "If anybody's shadowing us, he's had plenty of time to go past. We'll assume he spotted us smooching in the car."

"Kroch knows what you are," Olivia interrupted. "The passionate love scene isn't likely to have fooled him, is it? Any more than our hasty marriage?"

I said, watching her, "Let's not go overboard on this Kroch theory, Doc. He's our best bet, true, but he's acting very oddly. And if there should be somebody else, neither Kroch nor Mooney—"

She frowned quickly. "Who?"

"I don't know," I said. "But there's something in this damn case that I'm overlooking, and until I find it I'm not going to settle on Herr Kroch to the exclusion of everything else. And if it's Kroch following us, no harm is done. He'll naturally have some doubts about the sincerity of our display of passion; he'll wonder just who the hell we think we're fooling. He'll be puzzled. So much the better. He'll have all the more reason to want to find out what we're really up to in here. Let's hope he parks up ahead and comes sneaking back for a look. If he does, your job is to make him think we're both right here in this thicket. I leave the details to your imagination." I paused, and took my compact .38 Special out of my pocket. "One more thing. Have you ever been checked out on one of these, Doc?"

She shook her head. "No. Do I have to—"

"Something could go wrong. I was told you were valuable government property out on loan to us, to be returned in good condition. If there's trouble, I want you to have this."

"What about you?"

"Hell, I can't use a gun on him. I have to take him alive. But he's tough and experienced and he could get away from me and come for you. That's what the gun is for. It sounds like the crack of doom and it kicks like Tennessee white lightning, so hold it with both hands and don't let the uproar scare you. It holds five shots. Point it where you want to shoot and pull the trigger five times and once more for luck. Don't sit around waiting to see what the first shot will do. Just keep shooting till it clicks empty. Okay?"

She licked her lips, took the gun gingerly, and looked it over. "Okay, Paul. Where's the safety?"

I said, "You've been reading too many books, Doc. This is a revolver. If it had a safety I'd have told you. All you have to do is pull the trigger. Don't talk, don't threaten, don't warn, don't hesitate, just shove the thing out ahead of you and open up. *If* he comes in here after you. That'll mean I wasn't as good in the woods as I thought. You can't take him alone so don't try. But remember, we want him alive if it can possibly be arranged so don't shoot unless he's really coming for you." I started to turn away and stopped. "Just one more thing. We also want me alive if it can be arranged. At least I do. I'll sing out before I get too close. The password is still 'flattop.' Don't get nervous and blow my head off by mistake."

"I... I'll be careful." Her voice was a little shaky.

"Scared?" I asked.

She smiled faintly. "Just a little. Do you think he'll really come?"

"If there is a shadow—Kroch or somebody else—and if he gets curious enough, he'll come," I said. "If. That's one question. How far he'll come is another. We'll give it a full hour. Go into your act if you hear somebody out here."

I looked at her sitting on my spread-out coat, looking lost and out of place in the woods in her smart jersey dress—her wedding dress, as things had turned out— and her nylons and high heels, with the murderous little revolver in her hands. I found myself remembering, for some reason, Harold Mooney, the man she claimed to love, screaming silently into the twisted towel as she went into his arm without anesthetic. *I'm not a very nice person,* she'd said.

"Well, take it easy, Doc," I said, and slipped away.

He took forty-seven minutes to make up his mind, counting from the moment I left her. Lying in damp pine needles with a downed tree for shelter, I saw him coming, moving silently through the woods at the edge of the highway. It was Kroch, all right. So much for my fancy theories.

Anyway, he thought he was moving silently, but he didn't really like it and wasn't very good at it. Basically, I could see, he was a city man, a street man, a dark-alley man. He liked traffic, he liked cars, he liked shadowy doorways and narrow stairs. He liked abusing little girls in attic studios.

He didn't like trees and brush and pine needles and the soft uneasy murmur of the wind and the nervous chattering of a squirrel somewhere in the distance. The cawing of a lone crow cruising by at treetop height made him freeze and wait until he'd identified the sound by spotting the flying bird. A crow, for God's sake. You'd think anybody'd know a crow.

I lay behind my log and watched him and knew it wasn't going to work. He was acting too wary; he wasn't going to come in far enough to let me deal with him without risking interference from the highway. He'd seen the empty car but he was too smart to go near it. He was Karl Kroch and he'd had traps set for him before. He knew I was somewhere around, waiting.

He'd thrown me a challenge in New Orleans, to be sure; he'd sent me his name and a vainglorious message via Antoinette Vail. It was kid stuff, but it didn't mean he was going to give me any careless breaks in the showdown. He knew this wasn't the right place for him.

I'd picked the terrain, therefore I must like it. He didn't. To hell with Olivia Mariassy and the shadowing job, for the time being. To hell with me.

He turned and went back the way he'd come. Well, it had been a lot to hope for. Presently I heard a car start up in the distance and drive away. I was supposed to hear that. I didn't think he'd be going far.

I got up and brushed myself off and went back to the patch of bushes with the pine tree growing out of it. Olivia must have heard me coming because her voice reached me, low but audible: "Darling, please! How do you expect me to get my dress back on if you... Ah, don't, that tickles!" She laughed softly.

"Coming in," I said. "Flattop, like in aircraft carrier."

She was silent. I went in through the brush and found her sitting on my coat as I'd left her, fully dressed of course, holding the gun with both hands. It was aimed right at my chest. I stood quite still until the muzzle dropped.

She laughed again, a little embarrassed. "I thought it might be... You told me to go into my act if I heard somebody."

"Sure."

"Did you... what happened? Did you see anybody?"

"Yes, I saw him."

She looked up quickly. "Who?"

"It was Kroch after all," I said. "Maybe we've proved something. But he didn't like the setup. He sensed something wrong and flared off like a duck."

"So it's still left to be done." She drew a long breath

and rose and looked down at the gun in her hand. "You'd better carry this, hadn't you?" she said, giving it to me. She watched me start to put it away. "Paul?"

"Yes?"

"I'd like you to show me how to open it."

I hesitated. She was watching me with an odd kind of intentness. I said, "Sure," and brought the weapon out again. "You just use your thumb on the latch like this and the cylinder swings out… like this."

There was a little silence. She looked down at the weapon, open in my hand. She said quietly, "It isn't loaded, is it?"

"No," I said. "It isn't loaded, Doc." I took the cartridges from my pocket and started feeding them into the empty chambers.

"You weren't really trying to trap him, were you?"

I said, "I wanted to see if he was there. If he'd come in close, I'd have taken him if I could. I didn't really expect him to come in. It was too obvious a trap to catch a pro."

"But you were really testing me." Her voice was quite even. "Weren't you?"

I looked up from the gun. Her eyes met mine steadily. Even with the glasses on, they were pretty nice eyes. She was rather an attractive person, when she didn't have that grim, haggard, arrogant look, I reflected. Or maybe I was just getting used to her.

"You raised some disturbing possibilities with that last mysterious speech you made," I said. "I had to check them. Sooner or later I may have to turn my back on a loaded gun held by you, Doc, and I probably won't have time to worry about you then."

I expected her to be angry, or at least moderately resentful. To my surprise, she laughed, took a step forward and rose on tiptoe to kiss me on the mouth.

"You know, I could get quite fond of you, Corcoran or whatever your name is," she said, smiling. "You haven't an ounce of romance or chivalry in your makeup, and you don't know how refreshing that is to a lady who's been a sucker for moonlight and roses. Come on, let's go home. I'm going to make you carry me over the threshold for the benefit of the neighbors."

She did, too. It was a small, standardized house with a picture window in a development with winding streets laid out with a French curve by an architect who'd read in a magazine that straight streets were passé. Nevertheless, for a development, it didn't look too bad; and the house didn't look too bad, either, although I'm not really a picture-window man at heart. When we got inside, the phone was ringing.

15

I set her down inside the door and kicked it shut behind me. There wasn't anybody in here we needed to put on an act for, and the jangling telephone bell would have killed romance in any case, so I just stepped back and glanced at my watch. It read two o'clock. The little Renault was no sports machine and there had been some delays and detours so we hadn't made nearly the time covering the distance between New Orleans and Pensacola that young Braithwaite had managed in his racing Healey.

Olivia smoothed down her dress and went to the phone while I went back out for the suitcases. When I returned, she held the instrument out to me. I put my load down and took it.

"How's the honeymoon coming?" It was the familiar voice of the New Orleans contact I'd never met.

"Well," I said, "there's an old saw about three being a crowd, if you know what I mean."

"Who's your shadow, the great stone face?"

"That's right."

"Good. That just about clinches it. His being in New Orleans could have been some kind of coincidence, I suppose, but his trailing the lady across four states didn't happen by accident. He's our man, all right." There was a pause. "Is he around right now?"

"Well, he's not standing beside me," I said, "but I'd guess he's not too far away."

"That's nice," the man in New Orleans said. "That's nice because you're going to have to pick him up, it says here."

I didn't like the way he put it. I said carefully, "Sure, I know. As a matter of fact, I gave it half a try this afternoon, but Kroch's very cagey. I'm going to have to wait and set it up more carefully. Besides, the way the guy is acting bothers me. Half the time he's an experienced old pro and the other half he's a reckless, boastful punk. I'd like to find out what's behind his corny melodrama before I take him."

"You can ask him all the questions you want *after* you take him," said the voice on the phone. "But he followed Mariassy and nobody else did. Or did they?"

"No."

"Then he's the man you take, and you take him now. The Taussig matter is becoming urgent. Immediate action is requested, not to say commanded. Got it?"

I drew a long breath. "Sure. I got it."

"You take him. That's the word. I've got more good news for you. That little artist girl, the one with the attic studio and the black eye, came to the Montclair Hotel about half an hour after you left. She was looking for you."

"Antoinette Vail? What did she want?"

"She had a letter for you. When she was told at the desk that you'd checked out, she wanted to have it sent after you, but you'd left no forwarding address and we hadn't anticipated this possibility and tipped off the desk clerk, so he wouldn't take it. So we still don't know what the communication was, but by the looks of things you'll soon have an opportunity to find out."

"I will?" I said. "How?"

"While she was trying to learn how to reach you, who should appear but a certain Dr. Mooney, looking pale and favoring his left arm. Who's responsible? Your report is eagerly awaited. Anyway, he heard her asking questions about you. He had an idea. He approached her. She started to brush him off, but something he said caught her interest and they went up to his room to talk. A little later, very friendly, they drove off together in his car—a light blue Chrysler convertible, if it matters. She was driving, presumably because of his arm. Time of departure, ten-fifteen. Course, due east, Pensacola-wards. Speed, excessive. So you can expect company soon, you lucky boy."

"I see." I frowned. "And you have no idea what it is the girl wants to tell me."

"Not any."

"Damn," I said. "Can you have her picked up?"

"For what reason? On what charge?"

"Hell, have the cops pick them both up on the Mann

Act or something. They'll be crossing plenty of state lines between there and here."

"And this will accomplish what?"

"It will get the fool kid off the street before she gets herself clobbered again," I said.

"I don't think Washington is interested in getting fool kids off the street, friend," said the man in New Orleans. "Not enough to risk the publicity involved in pulling in a respectable Pensacola physician for associating with a pretty New Orleans artist. Can't you see the papers? And the girl has kept her mouth shut so far, but who knows what she'll do if we put her face to face with a lot of policemen and reporters asking questions. No, better let her come through. You handle her when she gets there. And find out what her urgent message is. After all, if it's important enough for her to write you a letter, it's important enough for us to know. Maybe she's remembered something about Kroch from last night, something she forgot to tell you."

He was right, of course. I said, "All right. But it's going to be a hell of a honeymoon."

The man in New Orleans laughed. "Your wife will understand. That's more than mine does. Well, you're out of my territory now. I'm switching you over to local control. You'll make contact at the Flamingo Lounge. Your bride can tell you where, or consult the city directory. Use the men's room routine. The urge to wash your hands will strike you at five-thirty sharp. The time is now two-oh-four."

I checked my watch. "Description?"

"You'll know him when you see him," said the voice on the phone. "There's an I-team standing by. Your contact will tell you how to whistle them up when you have the patient ready for the operation. Or you can do the work yourself, but rockface is to be captured, taken apart, and made to talk, soon. That's the word marked final."

There was nothing for me to say except, "Transmission received and acknowledged."

I heard a click and put the phone down, wondering if I'd ever met the man who'd called. Probably not. I looked up to see Olivia watching me, obviously puzzled and disturbed by what she'd heard.

"The Flamingo Lounge," I said.

"It's in the middle of town," she said.

"Driving time?"

"You'd better give yourself at least half an hour. Pensacola is bigger than it looks from the road we arrived on."

"Do you know the place?"

"Well… yes, I know it," she said after a brief hesitation. "It's right around the corner from Harold's office. We sometimes used to meet there for lunch or a drink before dinner."

"Can you tell me where the men's room is located?"

She glanced at me sharply to see if I was joking. She said, "Both rest rooms are to the left as you come in, back in the corner. You're going to meet somebody there?" When I nodded, she asked, "Am I going with you?"

"Not to the final rendezvous," I said. "It might cause comment. But as far as the lounge itself, yes. I wouldn't leave my bride home alone on our wedding night, would I? Besides, the last time we separated you wound up facing a man with a gun." I shook my head irritably. "I wish I knew for sure that Kroch is really as cocky and irresponsible and erratic as he acts."

Olivia was watching me steadily. "What's wrong, Paul? What did that man tell you on the phone?"

"Everything's wrong," I said. "Time seems to be running out on us, for one thing. Washington is jittery and screaming for immediate action; I've got orders to pick up Kroch at once, regardless. Well, as soon as I've conferred with some local guy I'm to meet at five-thirty. And just to make things real complicated, Antoinette Vail, the girl who got mussed up last night because I bought her a dinner, is heading this way with a mysterious letter in her hot little hand, intended for me. She's driving your friend Mooney's car, and he's right beside her. What he thinks he's doing, God only knows, but I'm sure it's clever as hell. I'm getting damn sick and tired of devious and clever people, Doc. I wish I could meet just one direct, stupid slob on this job—besides me, I mean."

Olivia laughed. "I don't recognize you from the description, Paul." After a moment she went on, "You're worried about the girl, aren't you? I gathered that much from what you said on the phone."

"Well, I dragged her into this," I said. "She's just a kid.

She's probably still got some kind of glamorous, juvenile notions about this business. Well, to hell with her. I can't be responsible for every crazy little girl who wants to play Mata Hari or something."

After a moment, Olivia turned away. I followed her into the next room, a living room. It had books along the walls—lots of books, a record player and records, and some furniture that looked comfortable but not particularly new or expensive. The only intriguing piece was a nice little table with a built-in chessboard upon which the men were set up, ready for a game. I remembered that I hadn't got very far into Capablanca.

Olivia wasn't in sight, but she soon came back through a swinging door that apparently led to the kitchen. A nook at that end of the room served as a dining alcove. She had a glass in each hand. I took one and raised it to her.

"To Mr. and Mrs. Corcoran," I said. We drank, and I looked at her for a moment. It was quiet and peaceful in the little house, and she was kind of a pleasant person to have around, and I was tired of thinking about Kroch and Antoinette Vail and my orders. Thinking wasn't getting me anywhere, and I said, "We have a couple of hours to kill, Doc, before we head for the Flamingo. I have a suggestion to make. It's subject to veto; I'm not pushing it; but I have a sudden urge to lock the doors and windows of the bridal cottage and consummate this crazy marriage. What do you say?"

She was silent. I saw that I had shocked her. "You put it crudely, Paul," she murmured at last. "I mean... well, we had the excuse of being rather drunk last night, but we're not drunk now."

I said, "It was just a suggestion. We can play chess instead. That was your original idea, remember?"

She smiled faintly, but the smile died at once. "I... I don't think I want to be made love to just to kill time. Besides, it's broad daylight and I've never... I don't know if I really could. No, I'd rather not."

"Sure," I said. "Well, if you're going to change clothes for this evening excursion, put on something dark, not too tight in the skirt, not too high in the heels."

She said, "I don't mean to be difficult or overly finicky. But there should be something more to it, shouldn't there? Not love necessarily, I don't mean that. Just so there's something."

I said, "You'll need this," and took the .38 Smith and Wesson out of my pocket. "That is to say, you may need it."

After a moment she reached for the gun. I flicked it open and laid it in her hand that way.

"As you can see, this time it's loaded," I said. "Those round brass things are the cartridge heads. You can kill five men with that, Doc, more if you line them up and shoot through two or three at a time, and don't think it won't. The brassiere is supposed to be a good place, or the top of the stocking. The purse is not so good; you may lay it down somewhere or have it snatched from you. Use your imagination. Whatever happens from now on, don't go anywhere without this gun, not even to the john. And remember what I told you, if you have to use it."

"I'll do my best if it's necessary," she said, rather uncertainly. "But you'll forgive my hoping I won't have to."

"Sure. There's another possibility," I said. "We don't know just how this will break. In the juvenile gangs, I understand, the girl generally carries the rod so the boy will be clean if he's frisked by the fuzz—police to you. If we should get in a bind together, I might want this back, very secretly and suddenly. Your signal is when I wiggle my ears like this... What's so funny?"

She was smiling. She looked down at the blunt, business-like little revolver and stopped smiling. "All right. When you wiggle your ears..." She broke up again.

"It may be funny now," I said severely. "It won't be when and if the time comes."

"I know," she murmured. "I'm just being silly."

I grinned. "You're a pretty good soldier, Doc."

"You don't know that yet," she said.

"I'm sorry if I stepped out of line," I said.

She hesitated for as long as a couple of seconds. Then she looked up at me. "But it wasn't out of line," she said in an even tone. "I was the one who was out of line, Paul. I forfeited all right to be prudish last night—and after all, we're married. Your request was perfectly legitimate."

I said, "Doc—"

"No," she said. "I've been protesting very loudly that I've had enough of romance and sentimentality and that I approved your lack of it. Why should I expect you to dress up your very sensible suggestion with tinsel flowers, like a lovesick boy? Just put my suitcase in the big bedroom and give me five minutes, Paul."

She started to turn away. I caught her aim and swung her back to face me. I said, "If you're trying to make me feel like a damn lecher—"

Then I stopped, because there were tears in her eyes. We looked at each other for a moment. I reached out and took the gun she was holding and put it on a nearby table. I took off her glasses and laid them beside the gun. She stood quite still while I was doing this. I kissed her carefully. Her arms went around my neck, and I kissed her again with less restraint.

We'd both been under strain of one kind or another for quite a while; we were both fed up with one thing and another, including ourselves, I guess. There comes a time when you need another human being for reasons that have very little to do with love.

She freed herself breathlessly at last. "No, darling, leave my dress alone. Maybe some other time you can rape me on the living room sofa. Today we'll use the bedroom like respectable married folks. Just… just wait here a minute, like a good boy, while I slip into something nice and sexy."

"Well, I'll wait," I said.

16

The Flamingo Lounge was located in the base of a tall new building on a wide boulevard with palms down the middle. Even after all the times I've been in California and Florida, not to mention the great Southwest, I can never quite get used to the idea of palm trees growing in the United States of America. They still look exotic and foreign to me, and I expect to hear natives beating on drums at night and lions growling in the bush. There was a parking lot across the street. I put the Renault into a vacant slot and went around to help my bride out.

There was some constraint between us. This business was no longer all playacting, but neither was it all for real. It was an uneasy, artificial relationship and I guess we were both aware that there would be a good deal to straighten out once the job was over, assuming we were both around to straighten it out afterward, and that it could be straightened.

She was wearing another good, smart, reasonably

expensive dress that might have upped the circulation of
Vogue slightly but did nothing much for her. It was dark
brown wool, a tunic job. I looked her over for bulges and
spotted none that weren't natural.

"Where is it?" I asked.

She laughed and touched her side where the tunic was
loose. "It's tucked into the top of my skirt," she said. "I'm
praying it doesn't fall through and go clattering on the
floor at an inopportune moment." She made a face. "You
can tell your information that the brassiere is a highly
overrated place of concealment for anybody who isn't
built like a Jersey cow; and I ruined a perfectly good
stocking trying to hide it down there."

I said, "Sure. Well, we're in good time, but we might
as well go over… Damn!"

"What's the matter?"

We were walking out of the lot. I'd been checking the
parked cars routinely. Now I stopped, looking down at a
low, racy, red topless job with big wire wheels. I knew it,
of course. I'd ridden in it to New Orleans and back. *You'll
know him when you see him,* the man on the phone had
told me cryptically.

"What is it, Paul?" Olivia asked.

"Nothing," I said. "Nothing, but I wish they'd just let
the kids play with their damn marbles and leave the dirty
work to us grown-ups. Come on."

At five-twenty, it was still daylight outside, but in the
Flamingo it was a cloudy and moonless midnight. We had to
pause for a moment to let our eyes get used to the blackness.

"No," Olivia said suddenly. Her fingers tightened on my arm.

"What's your problem?" I asked.

"That blonde. At the bar."

I didn't rubberneck. "So there's a blonde at the bar. Think I'm going to start chasing her?"

"She's Harold's nurse. Receptionist. You know the one. I told you. The one who laughed."

"Well, you said it was right around the corner from the office. Maybe she's stopping for a quick one on her way home. Maybe she needs it after answering the phone all day and telling the yearning ladies Dr. Kildare's out of town."

Olivia was gripping my arm hard. "I don't think I can stay in the same room with her, Paul. I'll either get deathly sick or attack her."

"Only men attack women," I said. "In one sense of the word, at least. And you're faking, Doc. Nobody hates nobody so much they can't keep their lunch down."

After a moment, she laughed. "Oh, dear. Can't I even exaggerate a *little?*"

"Not on duty," I said. "Tell me more."

"She must have stopped on her way home, as you say. She's still in her uniform."

"The transparent white nylon one?"

"With the pink undies showing through. Not to mention where the undies aren't. She's got a good-looking boy with her, standard TV model, nicely tanned, with wavy brown hair and flashing white teeth. He's in civilian clothes, sport coat and slacks, but he wears them like a uniform: I think he's Navy, from the base, off duty, probably an aviator. The airplane sailors have a slightly different look from the ship sailors. After a while at Pensacola you can distinguish them pretty well. Harold would be green with jealousy if he knew his little office queen was stepping out with a younger man."

I turned my head casually. It was Braithwaite, of course. It figured. After all, I had requested further information on Mooney. *Put somebody to really digging for dirt,* I'd said. *Cover his background, his home, his office...* How the Navy boy had got the job of approaching Mooney's nurse wasn't immediately clear, but it wasn't likely they'd met by accident.

She was young and quite pretty, I saw. Well, she would be. With Mooney's record for philandering, he'd hardly pick a hag to share his office hours. I remembered being told the turnover was considerable.

The current incumbent had her nurse's cap perched on a piled-up mass of pale hair that made her look a little top-heavy. It seemed like a lot of hairdo to take to work every day. She was slightly plump for my taste, sticking out rather obviously and spectacularly in front, but the waist was small and the arms seemed to be nicely proportioned inside the semitransparent sleeves of her uniform. The white stockings and sturdy, low-heeled white shoes couldn't hide the fact that the round calves and trim ankles would pass inspection anywhere.

"You've got a good eye, Doc," I said. "He is Navy and he is a fly-boy."

"That's not where you're looking," Olivia said dryly. "But since you know him, I suppose he's the one you came here to meet."

"Maybe. He's obviously got one job already. We'll see if he has two." I glanced surreptitiously at my watch. "Let's grab a booth. You don't want to be left standing when nature calls me, a hundred and forty-three seconds from now."

I seated her at the side of the room. She started pulling off her gloves, glancing toward the young couple at the bar.

"I don't understand... Oh. He's trying to get her to tell him things about Harold for you, I suppose. Well, he's come to the right person. She should have a lot of fascinating information on the subject."

"Let's hope she does," I said, and then it was time to go. I rose and said in clear, husbandly tones: "Order me a bourbon and water, dear, if you can catch a waiter. I'll be right back."

I didn't look toward the bar as I went off, but I was aware that Braithwaite was still engrossed in his conversation with the blonde girl in medical white. Either he'd forgotten, or he wasn't my man after all, or our watches were out of sync, or his time had been set a minute or two later than mine. I entered the tiled precincts and stalled a little in the obvious way. When I turned to wash my hands, he was there, washing his hands. We were alone in the place.

I said, "Go ahead."

"The interrogation team is in town. I have the address

and telephone number written down—"

"Never write anything down. Give it here."

He tore a leaf from a small notebook and passed it over. I memorized the information and flushed the paper down the nearest john.

"How much do you know?" I asked the boy.

"Enough, I think, sir. Have you spotted your man yet?"

"I have a man spotted. Orders are to take him. Never mind that. You saw the lady with me? Well, you probably recognized her from the ship. Dr. Mariassy."

"Yes, sir."

"If I get busy and things look rough, I may have to unload her on you. As far as you're concerned, she is not expendable. You will keep her alive and unhurt if you have to stop the bullets and knives with your own head or heart, whichever you consider more impenetrable. Communication understood?"

"Yes, sir."

"Are you armed?"

"Yes, sir."

"Can you shoot?"

"Yes, sir."

That probably meant he wasn't very good, I reflected, looking at him sourly; and if he was good at all it was probably only on paper targets. The Navy doesn't go in for small arms much—they figure on the Marines doing the shooting—and there are all degrees and kinds of marksmanship. No man who really knows how to shoot is going to answer that question without qualification. Well, it was the best arrangement I could make at the moment.

"Where can I reach you if I need you tonight?" I asked. "You're not still living aboard the training carrier, I hope."

"No, sir. I'm staying temporarily at the BOQ on the base."

"Phone?"

"Well, there's no room phone, but if you call the building—"

"Hell, I can't go through all that," I said impatiently. "And I can't send a lady to visit you in the Bachelor Officers' Quarters, either." I frowned. "What about this nurse? Does she live alone?"

"I believe so, sir."

"How far have you got with her? Do you think she may ask you to her place if you play it right? Since you obviously can't ask her to yours?"

He flushed slightly. "Well, sir, I... I think so. She's very friendly. I was going to ask you. I mean, I'm not a kid or anything, but I didn't know how far... I mean, they didn't tell me if I was really supposed to..."

I said, "I want you to spend the night with her, so I know where I have you if I need you. That will also give you an opportunity to carry out your primary mission, which I presume is gathering information about her employer. Whatever else you do or don't do is up to you, as long as you keep her friendly and unsuspicious."

He hesitated. "Yes, sir," he said reluctantly.

"Objection?"

"There's hardly any alternative, is there, sir? And,

well, it just seems a little cold-blooded."

I was reminded of Olivia's attitude of a couple of hours ago. I suppose it should have given me a warm and sentimental feeling to know there were still people around for whom sex had a symbolic significance, but I'll have to admit that it merely made me impatient.

"Jesus," I said, "a Navy man with a conscience about dames? I thought you fellows had girls in every port."

He drew himself up. "I've had plenty of girls, sir! It's not that. Only, well, she seems like a nice kid—"

The damn case seemed to be crawling with nice kids. "You think she's a nice kid but you think she'll go to bed with you," I said. "Well, I'll give you a hint. If you simply can't bear to lay the young lady under false pretenses, just make like you're drunk and pass out on the floor. If she's really a nice kid, and even if she isn't, she'll probably just drag you to the couch and leave you to sleep it off. She may even make coffee for you in the morning. Okay?"

"Yes, sir. I'm sorry, I didn't mean—"

"Has she come out with any information of interest about Dr. Mooney?"

"Not much. I haven't really dared try to pump her yet. After all, I only picked her up… made contact with her at lunch. From what she says, the doctor is kind of an amorous slob and keeps her dodging. The previous girl quit, Dottie says, because she'd worn out her track shoes; that kind of stuff. Mooney tells Dottie about his affairs with other women and hints that she could share the bliss if she wanted. So far, she says, she hasn't wanted, but it's hard work. She's considering getting another job, but he pays well."

I said, "That corresponds with information received, up to a point. My dope is that she isn't quite as innocent, Mooney-wise, as you make her sound. But my informant was prejudiced."

Braithwaite shook his head quickly. "I think Dottie's telling the truth. She's… well, she really seems like a swell kid, sir. I'd hate to think I was dragging her into anything…" He stopped.

I looked at him, and thought for some reason of a swell kid I'd dragged into the case, sobbing into a damp pillow. I asked, "What's your first name, Mr. Braithwaite?"

"Why… why, it's Jack, sir."

"Well, Jack," I said, "some day you may have to fire off those big Navy guns of yours, or drop those big bombs, and some people are going to get hurt who maybe aren't as guilty as some other people. Maybe there'll be some who aren't guilty at all. And do you know, it'll be just too damn bad, Jack."

He said stiffly, "Yes, sir."

"How'd you get roped into this?" I asked.

"I wasn't roped in," he protested. "I volunteered, sir, as you told me I could. I called the number you gave me in Washington. They called me back almost immediately. They're going to put me through some special training—you know more about that than I do, sir—but this thing was breaking fast and they had nobody else available locally. Besides, I'd already been in on it, a little. I knew you by sight."

"Sure," I said. "In the Army we used to distinguish between three classes of fools: the plain fools, the damn fools, and the volunteers." Staring at him coldly, I saw his jaw muscles work a little, but he'd been hazed before. He had discipline. He didn't talk back. He was a pretty good boy, but I wasn't about to let him know I thought so. He'd work better under strain. I went on, "The nurse's name is Darden, isn't it? Where does she live?"

He brought out the notebook again. I ripped the page out and disposed of it as before, after memorizing the data written on it.

"If she'd seen that," I said, "she'd have thought it was mighty damn funny your having it written down before she'd ever told you."

"Yes, sir."

"I don't really mean to give you a hard time, Jack."

"No, sir."

"I wouldn't expect to fly an airplane without plenty of training, but that's just about what you're going to have to do here. And a mistake in this business can be just as fatal to just as many people, or more."

"Yes, sir."

"All right," I said. "Give me a minute before you come out."

I straightened my tie at the mirror and went out, leaving him there. As I emerged from the corner devoted to the rest rooms I saw Dottie Darden standing at the booth talking earnestly to Olivia, whose face looked pale and hostile. The kid was obviously trying to sell her something and she just as obviously wasn't buying.

"Please," Dottie was saying as I came up. "I'd like you to understand, Dr. Mariassy. I know you think I'm terrible and I don't blame you, but after all, he *is* my employer. I *have* to listen to his stories and pretend to laugh. I have to keep him happy."

"Yes, I'm sure you're very good at that," Olivia said. "I'm sure you keep him very happy."

The nurse winced. "If it makes you feel better to be jealous of me, go right ahead," she said. "You've got lots of company. Half the women in town would like to scratch my eyes out; and the funny thing is, I wouldn't touch that creep with rubber gloves on. Honest." She drew a sharp breath. "But you won't believe that. Nobody'll believe that. I'm sorry. I just wanted to apologize." She turned quickly and almost ran me down. I had to catch her to keep her from falling. She looked up at me, startled, looking very soft and young in the dimly lighted lounge, with her ridiculously formal coiffure contrasting oddly with her plain white uniform.

"Oh, I'm sorry," she gasped, freeing herself.

Braithwaite was returning. She went to him quickly, pulled herself together, and answered his puzzled question with a laugh and a shake of the head. I sat down. Olivia was staring grimly at her glass.

I took a drink from mine, standing there untouched, and said, "You were a little tough on the kid, weren't you?"

"Kid?" she snapped. "They're all kids to you, aren't they, Paul? But if she's really the innocent child she pretends, would she flaunt her pectoral development like that? If it's really hers, and particularly if it isn't."

"Pectoral," I said. "I'll have to remember that. When I was a boy, we simply called them boobs. Pectoral development sounds much more refined."

Olivia looked up. After a moment she laughed. Braithwaite was leaving, taking with him the nurse and his tender conscience. I'd had one once, I remembered—a conscience, I mean—but I'd managed to lose it somewhere. At least I'd done my best to. In this business a conscience buys you nothing but trouble.

17

"There's the bridge," Olivia said. "Are we driving over to the island?"

I looked at the long causeway ahead, then glanced at the rearview mirror. It was quite empty, as far as significant images were concerned.

"There's no point going out there and getting our shoes full of sand if nobody's interested," I said, pulling out where we could see the water. "Of course, Kroch could still be tailing us, but I don't have quite the right itch between my shoulder blades. I think, now that he's got you established in Pensacola again, he's let you go for a little, figuring he can always pick you up at the house or the naval base."

She shivered slightly. "When he wants me," she murmured. "When he gets his orders to kill me. It's like living in a different world, knowing there are men like that."

"Yeah," I said. "We affect people adversely, we

professionals. Why, some girls won't even be seen talking to us."

She said quickly, "I didn't mean—"

"I know what you meant."

"You're not like Kroch."

I said, "Cut it out, Doc. How do you know? You've never spoken to Kroch except for a moment in your hotel room when he was holding a gun and doing most of the talking. You've never been to bed with him. Hell, he might be a perfectly swell guy in bed. How do you know?"

She said stiffly, "That isn't funny; and you're being ridiculous, comparing yourself with a thug like that."

I said, "You're the one who's being ridiculous, Doc. You're trying to make a fine moral distinction between a man you happen to dislike and a man you happen to like—if I may flatter myself—both of whom happen to be engaged in exactly the same type of work."

She was silent for a little; then she smiled and said, "Well, have it your way. I'm married to a monster without any relieving traits."

"That's what I'm trying to tell you," I said. I looked out over the water at the low black mass of land at the end of the bridge. "Give me the details. What's it like out there? I've seen it from the air, that's all."

She'd have preferred to keep the conversation personal, I saw, but she said, "It's a narrow barrier island, just a sandspit, running parallel to the coast a mile or so out. To the west, the right as you come off the bridge, it extends only a few miles. There's an old brick Civil War fort at that end, and some deserted concrete structures that used to house big coast-defense guns—relatively modern, I believe, but the guns have been removed. That end of the island is a state park. The other way, eastwards, to the left as you come off the bridge, there's a little beach community and then nothing much but road and sand dunes for thirty-some miles. Another bridge over there brings you back to the mainland. The island goes on to the east still farther, I think, but I've never been there."

"You draw a good picture, Doc," I said. "Very sharp and clear."

"I ought to," she said. "It's part of my job to make things sharp and clear." After a little, she said, "If we're through here, I'd like to go home."

"Sure."

I started the car and drove slowly back through town. The housing development in which she lived had the clean, phony look of a movie set before the crew has got it convincingly weathered and dusty. I parked in front of her house.

"Paul," she said as I started to get out.

"Yes?"

"The divorce," she said. "I hate to be practical, but just how will it be arranged?"

"The legal department will take care of it." I guess I hadn't expected her to bring up the subject, although there was no reason why she shouldn't. "They're very efficient," I said. "They'll discover that we're absolutely incompatible, or something. Okay?"

"Don't be angry," she said. "I just wanted to know."

"Who's angry?"

"You sounded annoyed." She hesitated. "If it will make you feel better, I can tell you that I don't feel very incompatible." She glanced at me quickly and looked away. "In fact if… It's a brazen thing to say, I suppose, but I'm rather tired of pretending to be discreet and modest. If you would care to try to work something out without the legal department, afterward, the lady might be willing."

I looked at her, and closed the car door I'd just opened. I started to speak. She shook her head quickly.

"No, don't say anything and don't stare at me, please. This isn't a declaration of undying love, Paul. All I'm saying is that you seem to be a reasonably civilized person in spite of your weird occupation. Maybe you'd like to have a secret home base, a place to rest between assignments, under a name that isn't yours, a name like Corcoran, say. As for me, well, my one amorous adventure didn't turn out very well and I have a full time occupation that really interests me very much. Still, I… well, let's just say I wouldn't mind having you around the house occasionally. It might be a very practical arrangement for both of us." She shook her head again as I tried to interrupt. "No, I don't want you to say anything now. I just wanted to place my attitude on record. Anyway, I think the telephone is ringing."

I started to speak again, but now I could hear the bell, too, through an open window. I drew a long breath, then got out and followed her up the walk to the door and waited while she found the key to let us in. She went quickly to the phone. I saw her face go pale as she listened. She looked at me, muffling the mouthpiece with her hand.

"It's a man. I… I think I recognize the voice. But he wants a Mr. Helm, a Mr. Matthew Helm. Is that you?"

I sighed. It had been lots of fun playing house, but you've got to grow up some time and face the realities of the big cruel world.

"That's me," I said and took the phone from her. "Corcoran here," I said. "Helm, if you prefer."

"Good evening, Eric," Kroch's voice said in my ear. I knew it was his voice although I'd never heard it. That seemed strange. I felt as if I'd known him for years.

"So you know the code name, too," I said. "Hurray for you."

"I'm Kroch," he said. "Karl Kroch. But you know. The little girl told you."

"She told me," I said.

"I have her here," he said. "Miss Antoinette Vail."

The house seemed suddenly chilly, perhaps because of the open window. I said "Jesus Christ, has that stupid little chick gone and got herself loused up again? I tell you what you do, Kroch, just tie a good big rock around her neck and throw her off the nearest pier as a favor to me. Okay?" I saw Olivia's eyes widen, shocked.

"Very good, Eric." Kroch laughed softly in my ear. "Very good. That is the proper reaction. I am to think

Miss Vail means nothing to you, *hein?*"

I said, "Hell, I never saw her before the other night. What's she supposed to mean?"

"If you're willing to sacrifice her, of course, there is no more to be said. But if you are not... Do you know Santa Rosa Island? Of course you do. You were just looking at it across the water."

So the itch between my shoulder blades had let me down. I said, "A man stops to look at the water and talk to his wife. Big deal. And what's with this sacrifice bit? I told you, the kid's nothing to me. I needed a dame, or thought I did, so I picked her up at the bar. That's all. And I've been at this work too long to stick my neck out for innocent bystanders, Kroch. She's all yours. If you're hungry, stick an apple in her mouth and roast her."

He laughed again. "Ah, but it is nice to deal with someone who knows how the game should be played! You make me very happy, Eric. Now, what do you say? It is the logical place to finish this, out there, is it not? Very quiet, very lonely. Turn right as you leave the bridge. You will come to a gatehouse. There is a chain across the road there; the state park is closed at night. Leave your car by the little house and walk down the road. Or crawl through the sand or sneak through the bushes. I will be waiting. I will not be foolish enough to tell you to come unarmed. Bring all the weapons you wish. You will, anyway."

I said, "I told you, I've lost no little girls. She's all yours. What do you think I am, some kind of a Galahad or something? Cut her into little pieces and use her for bait."

Kroch laughed approvingly. I was still playing the game right. "The man, too?" he asked.

"What man?"

"There was a man in the car with Miss Vail. I was watching your house when the two of them drove up. I had no use for the man, but what could I do but bring him along? His name is Mooney. He has a big mouth. It has already got him shot once today; it could get him killed. Your little girl has a big mouth, too, but I will try to let you see her once more. I have a tender heart. Would you like to hear her voice?"

I didn't say anything. I heard a scuffle at the other end of the line; then Antoinette Vail was speaking breathlessly in my ear: "Mr. Corcoran, don't come, he'll kill you! Don't listen—"

Her voice was cut off. Kroch came back on. "That's right, Mr. Corcoran. If you come, I will kill you. Unless of course you kill me. Why don't you try?"

18

The apartment building in which Dorothy Darden lived was only a few blocks from the center of town. The red Austin-Healey sports job was parked at a meter up the street. I shoved Olivia out on the sidewalk, joined her and took her arm when she threatened to balk again. One day I'll do a job with a woman who has more sense than temperament. I'd thought that Dr. Olivia Mariassy, with her scientific background, might turn out to be the one. I'd been wrong.

"Just follow instructions like a good girl or I swear I'll bust you one," I said. "We haven't time for personalities."

She said, "I'm not going up there! I won't stay in the same place with that blonde tramp! I'd much rather be killed!"

"Nobody's interested in your 'druthers,'" I said. "Sorry, Doc, but that's the way it is. You go in there with your teeth or without them. Take your choice."

"You… you dictatorial beast!"

"Monster was the word we settled on," I said. "You'll go in and you'll ring the way I told you. Braithwaite has his orders concerning you. You may have a little wait while they get some clothes on and some lipstick off, depending on what stage in the proceedings you interrupt."

"Damn you, Paul—"

"Shut up," I said. "Listen closely. You'll tell Braithwaite that I'm going out to the island. Tell him that Kroch has the Vail kid and Dr. Mooney and is using them for bait, that tired old gag. I'm to turn right beyond the bridge, leave the car at the entrance to the park, and proceed on foot. Kroch will be waiting. He thinks he's Jim Bowie or something. He's in effect challenged me to single combat out on the sands. Maybe he really is nuts. Anyway, tell Jack Braithwaite, if he doesn't hear from me in an hour, he's to call in the team—he'll know what I mean—and come after me. When somebody says an hour, Doc, you look at your watch."

She started to speak angrily, checked herself, and glanced down. "Eleven thirty-three. Paul—"

"At twelve thirty-three the relief expedition gets under way. I don't want them to jump the gun. I want plenty of time out there. But when they come, tell them to beat the bushes hard, because their man will be there. If I'm in trouble, tell them. I'll use the needle on him. Injection C. It'll keep him anchored till they get there. If they're in a hurry to ask their questions, there's an antidote they can use. They'll know."

Some of her anger seemed to have evaporated. She

asked rather uncertainly, "And where will you be, Paul?"

"Who knows?" I shrugged. "As they say in what used to be my part of the country, *quién sabe*? Taking an armed man alive is always tricky. But I have everything working for me. He seems to be under the illusion he's Superman or Captain Blood or somebody. He also seems to have something on his mind, and five will get you twenty that he'll want to tell me all about it. A man who wants to talk has two strikes against him in a game like this. Furthermore, unless he's changed his style of armament, he's very lightly gunned. I should be able to reach him and immobilize him, one way or another. Your job is to see that Braithwaite sends out the wrecking crew to pick him up if I don't bring him in within the hour."

"You mean," she said, "if you're dead."

"Dead, wounded, or just plain tired. Why borrow trouble?"

"It sounds… it sounds absolutely suicidal to me! At least you should take a gun."

"He's got to talk," I said. "I can't risk using a gun, I might kill him. Here." I took the little knife from my pocket and held it out. "Keep this for me, too. I don't want any temptation around. It's going to be hard enough to keep from finishing him with my bare hands."

She looked at the knife and shivered slightly. "I didn't know you carried that, Paul. What a wicked, beautiful thing!"

"A present from a woman," I said. "You don't have to be jealous. She's dead." After a moment, I said, "I'm sorry I talked rough! I wasn't mad at you, not really. You know how it is."

"I know," she said. She looked up. "I'll deliver your message, of course, but I'd rather… Can't I go home afterward? I could take a taxi. I have your revolver. I'm sure I'd be perfectly safe at home."

I shook my head and led her into the building. The hallway was lined with pink marble and brass mailboxes. I checked the tenants' names, found the one I wanted, and turned to face Olivia.

"What makes you so sure you'd be safe?" I asked. "Suppose when I get out there Mr. Kroch isn't waiting on that lonely island beach like he promised. Suppose it's just a trick to get me away. Suppose the big bell is tolling, the great gong has been struck; suppose Emil Taussig has pressed the go-button and everywhere across the nation the shadowers are closing in on the people they've been trailing for weeks and months, waiting for this moment. Suppose Kroch has got the word. He knows I'm staying as close to you as your best girdle. I could create a problem—unless he can send me off to hunt lizards and frogs on Santa Rosa Island while he takes care of his business with you. Maybe he's been building up this screwy, aggressive, melodramatic character for just this moment, so I'd fall for the trick when the time came."

"But if you think that—"

"I don't think that," I said. "It's merely one of several possibilities."

Anger was back in her voice as she said sharply, "If you think it's even a possibility, why are you leaving me with an untrained boy and a blonde while you go chasing off to rescue—" She stopped abruptly. "I'm sorry. I suppose you do have to go after them. I suppose I even want you to."

I said, "You're a nice girl, Doc, but you're still very innocent, even after all the work I've done to bring you up right. You still believe everything you see on TV."

She frowned quickly. "What do you mean?"

"Nobody's going to rescue nobody," I said. The stone walls and metal mailboxes threw my voice back at me flat and hard. "Nobody's going to rescue Toni, Doc. Nobody's going to rescue Harold. Nobody's going to rescue them for the simple reason that they're dead."

There was a little silence. Somewhere in the building somebody had a radio going. It probably wasn't Braithwaite and the nurse. They'd be entertaining themselves in other ways. Olivia was staring at me, aghast.

"But—"

"They've been dead since Kroch hung up the phone," I said flatly, "unless it took him a few minutes to find a secluded spot to do the job. This isn't Hollywood, Doc. This is for real. Kroch had a use for them. Well, for one of them. He may have thought there was more between me and Toni than just a dinner at Antoine's, or he may just have hoped I was sentimental about young girls in general. In any case he wanted me to hear her voice so I'd know he wasn't bluffing."

"But... but that doesn't necessarily mean he killed them! Once he'd used the girl—"

"Once he'd used her, what could he do with her? Or with Mooney? Turn them loose to call the police?" I shook my head. "He wanted to be sure I'd come, whether or not he's going to be there himself. If he is, he wanted to be sure I'd come angry. An angry man is easier to deal with in most cases. There are exceptions, there are times when an angry man can be hard to stop, but he's not thinking of those. And when he no longer needed Toni... when he no longer needed them, he shot them. I know that and he knows I know it. It's one of the things he's counting on to make me come."

She licked her lips. "You're just guessing, Paul!"

I said, keeping my voice even, "They're lying out in the sand right now, or in the bushes, or in their car if he isn't expecting to use it. Or they're drifting out into the Gulf of Mexico on the tide, if there is a tide around here and it happens to be going out."

She said angrily, "You don't know. You can't *know!*" She wasn't even thinking of Mooney yet, and what his death might or might not mean to her. She simply didn't want to believe it could happen—that a couple of people could die casually because a man with a gun didn't want to be bothered, or wanted to bother somebody else.

"Of course I know," I said. "I know because it's what I would do—what any pro would do—with a couple of hostages that weren't needed any more. It's what I'd do if I were operating alone in enemy territory and had important work coming up, as Kroch is and has. Why bother to tie them and gag them and take a chance on their working loose and making trouble? That only happens in the movies, Doc. In real life, everybody knows that nobody makes trouble with a bullet through the head. Besides, as I said, Kroch wants to annoy me."

"Annoy," she breathed. "*Annoy!*"

I jerked my hand toward the mailboxes. "There it is. The name is Darden, as you know. The number is 205." I looked at her for a moment longer. "In case I run into trouble, or something, that chess book you once lent me is in my suitcase."

Then I was out of there and driving away, hoping I hadn't sounded too much like an ancient Greek promising to come back with his shield or on it. I hadn't the slightest intention of committing suicide if I could help it; and if you can't help it, it isn't suicide. It was going to be tricky, of course. An old pro like Kroch is always tricky, even with a screw loose; and bringing them back alive isn't as easy as shooting them, whether you're talking about elephants or enemy agents. Under the circumstances I'd much rather have brought him back dead, but that was a luxury duty said I must forego.

There wasn't any traffic on the causeway. If people lived all year in the little beach community Olivia had said was on the island, they apparently had no business on the mainland at this time of night. I crossed the sound and made the right turn as instructed, and soon there was nothing but sand on either side, irregular low dunes of it, with dark water showing occasionally beyond. The road was black against the white sand.

I saw the little gatehouse in the headlights and drove right up to it. There was nothing to be gained by being clever. He was expecting me to be clever. He was expecting me to pull off the road out of sight and sneak around like an Indian, all loaded down with lethal hardware. Since that was what he was expecting, I just drove up beside the car already parked at the side of the gatehouse and stopped.

It took me a little while to figure out how to turn on the interior lights of the Renault: you just twist the little plastic light itself. I took from my pocket the flat drug case we're all issued. It contains a special hypo and three types of injections, two permanent and one temporary. It also contains the little death pill for the agent's own use, unless he's wearing it elsewhere. I wasn't wearing mine on this job, since I didn't know anything of interest to anybody.

I loaded the hypodermic with the full four-hour dose of the temporary injection C, and put the stuff back into my pocket. I switched off the lights of the Renault and got out and looked around. The other car seemed to be a light blue in color. It was one of the big Chryslers, a convertible. That made it Mooney's, by the description I'd been given. Where Kroch's own car was hidden was anybody's guess. I didn't even know what make it was. He'd never given me a look at it. I reminded myself not to underestimate the guy. He might act loco at times, but his basic techniques were still good.

I thought about pulling the distributor heads off both cars, or bogging the vehicles in the sand somehow, but that would have been meeting him on his own terms, and he'd still have one car staked out somewhere in working condition. Instead, I left the key in the Renault, to make it look as if I didn't care how much transportation was available.

I went over to the road, stepped over the long, sagging, padlocked chain, and marched on toward the western end of the island, still a mile or so distant if Olivia had briefed me correctly. My shoes made loud noises on the hard pavement. The island was wider here—no longer just a strip of sand—and there were trees and bushes on both sides. The Gulf of Mexico was darkly visible off to my left. To my right, the water of the mile-wide sound I'd crossed couldn't be seen for a patch of woods, except where the trees had been cut away to allow for a half-overgrown road down to what seemed to be a rotting old pier.

I saw an oddly symmetrical, long, low, shadowy hill to the right of the main road and realized that it was man-made: a great structure of concrete covered with dirt and overgrown with grass and brush. It was close to a hundred yards long, with two black openings gaping seaward. There was a neat little state-park sign in front.

I went up and struck a match like a nocturnal sightseer, wondering where he was hiding and how eager his finger was on the trigger. Well, if he wanted to shoot, he'd shoot.

If not, if he really wanted to talk first, as I guessed, he'd be puzzled by my unorthodox behavior, which was fair enough. I'd been puzzled by his.

Apparently he wanted to talk first. No bullets came. The sign indicated that I was looking at the site of a former battery of two twelve-inch guns placed *en barbette*, whatever that might mean, in 1916, and casemated, whatever that might mean, in 1942.

He gave me no sign of his presence, but I knew he was watching as I blew out the match and waited for my eyes to get used to the darkness again. He'd be checking off one opportunity missed. He'd be wondering if maybe he shouldn't have shot after all, and to hell with conversation.

There were small night sounds all around. I wondered about snakes. It looked like good country for snakes and they always scare me. I started back toward the road and stopped. The farther opening in the gun emplacement or casemate or whatever it was showed a hint of light that hadn't been there earlier.

I don't suppose he really expected me to go right for it like a moth to a flame. He probably expected me to scout the whole deserted fortification first, looking for a back door by which I could sneak in and catch him by surprise—only he knew all the entrances and exits better than I did. He'd had time to learn them. Wherever I came in, he'd be waiting, so why waste the time?

I went straight for the lighted opening, therefore, and almost broke my leg stumbling into a masonry circle set in the ground in front, maybe something to do with the

traversing mechanism of the great coast-defense gun
that once had defended this shore of Florida first from
the Kaiser and then from Adolf Hitler. I couldn't help
wondering if they'd ever found anything to shoot at from
here—perhaps a periscope or two out in the Gulf, or what
looked like a periscope to an excited draftee.

The concrete doorway behind the circle was the size
of a railway-tunnel opening. The light was quite weak,
apparently only a reflection from a side corridor in there.
I went in. The tunnel went straight through the artificial
hill. I could see the vague shape of a smaller back entrance
with trees beyond. It was barred by a metal grill.

I came to the side corridor, a concrete passageway that
presumably ran the whole length of the fortification, but
I couldn't see much beyond the lighted doorway on the
right, just a few yards from the corner.

When I stood still, there wasn't a sound in the place
except the sound of my own breathing. When I turned and
walked toward the light, my footsteps awoke echoes all
through the man-made hill. I came to the doorway. The
room beyond might have been living quarters once, or
an ammunition storage space. Now it was just an empty,
windowless concrete chamber—almost empty, that is.

A kerosene lantern tied to a ringbolt in the far wall
threw a yellow light over the barren room. Two motionless
shapes were sprawled on the floor to one side. Well, I'd
predicted that.

I'd predicted it to Olivia, who hadn't wanted to believe
me, but I stood quite still anyway, regarding the two

bodies from the doorway. Mooney was in his slacks and tweedy sport coat. A snappy hat lay beside him. Toni was wearing a loose, heavy black sweater, tight black pants and little black shoes resembling ballet slippers. She could have been sleeping quietly with her face turned toward the wall, except that nobody normally goes to sleep fully dressed on the dusty, hard concrete floor of an abandoned fortification…

Even as I thought this, one of the figures moved. Mooney struggled to a sitting position, so that I could see that his hands and feet were tied; a tight gag kept him from crying out. He tried, however. He stared at me with bulging eyes and made some choked, gurgling noises, pleading for release I suppose. To hell with Harold Mooney.

I went forward, trying not to let myself feel hope, and knelt beside Toni. I put my hand on her shoulder and she seemed to move in response, rolling over on her back sleepily to see who'd disturbed her. Then I saw the blank, wide-open eyes in the pale, bruised face—and the little bullet-hole between the fine black eyebrows.

"Good evening, Eric," said Kroch's voice behind me.

19

I suppose it was a moment of triumph or something. I'd figured it right, hadn't I? I'd figured everything absolutely right, with the exception of Mooney's survival. The old crystal ball had been working pretty well. The man I wanted was within reach and I wasn't dead.

Everything was working out for me, just as I'd told Olivia. Hell, outfiguring a clumsy crumb like Kroch was just child's play for the brilliant, scheming mind of that old maestro of the undercover services, Matthew Helm. Now all I had to do was take him.

"Get up," Kroch said. "Be very careful, Eric."

"Shut up," I said without turning my head.

"Ah, yes," he said. "A moment for sentiment. Very well, but no tricks."

I looked down at the kid. There was some white paper sticking out of a pocket of her dusty black pants. I pulled it out. It was a crumpled envelope with my name written on it, or the name I was wearing currently: *Mr. Paul*

Corcoran, Montclair Hotel—please forward. I could feel Kroch watching me closely, but he didn't interfere as I opened the letter. It was not a letter, however. There was no writing inside. There were only three fifty-dollar bills.

There had never been any mysterious message, just the money I'd left in her studio, the money her pride and anger had forced her to try to return, preferably by finding me and throwing it in my face. And still at the end, I remembered, she'd tried to warn me off. *Mr. Corcoran, don't come,* she'd cried into the phone, *don't come, he'll kill you!*

"That's long enough," Kroch said. "The period of mourning is over. It is too bad. She was quite pretty. You have very good taste, Eric. The one in Redondo Beach, she was extremely attractive. It hurt me to have to send her off the road to her death. Such a waste. But if they will associate with people like us, they must take the risks, *hein?*"

There was suddenly a funny roaring sound in my ears, as if the beach had moved closer so that I could hear the surf.

"Gail?" I said. "You killed Gail Hendricks, too?"

"Was that her name?" he asked casually. "Didn't you know? Let us say she helped kill herself. She was really driving much too fast for the amount of alcohol she had consumed. Her reflexes were, shall we say, ragged. When I pulled alongside in the curve, very close, and blew my horn loudly... well, at that speed it takes very little to send a car out of control." He paused. "Surely you didn't think it was an accident. Accidents do not happen to people like us, Eric. You should know that."

He was right, of course. I should have known it, but there had been no indication at the scene of the wreck and no motive that I could think of. As murder, Gail's death still didn't make sense as part of the case. He'd killed her before I'd even been given the assignment, before anybody could know I was taking it, since I didn't even know it myself. I thought about this, or tried to think about it, but all that really came was the fact that he had killed her. That was two counts against Mr. Kroch. It was going to be very hard to keep him alive when the time came.

His voice came, easy and confident: "Well, so it goes. *So geht's im Leben*. All right, stand up. Put your hands against the wall. So."

Standing there, I felt his hands go over me. They found nothing of significance except the little case in my coat pocket. I felt that taken away.

"No weapons, Eric?" He sounded puzzled and rather disappointed.

"I stashed them," I said. "There's a tommy-gun hidden every five paces between here and the car."

"You hid nothing," he said. "I was watching. And they would do you no good out there, anyway. You are not going out there again. Turn around, slowly."

I turned and looked at him for the first time that night. He was standing well back so I couldn't grab the gun. He'd got no handsomer since the last time I'd seen him.

His clothes were rumpled and dirty and he needed a shave. The bald dome of his head looked startlingly smooth and shiny above the craggy, lined face with its rough chin.

The weapon in his hand looked like a Star, one of those Spanish automatics. It wasn't the smallest gun in the world—the shape of the cartridge, tiny though it is, makes it difficult for technical reasons to build a really small .22 automatic pistol—but it looked like a child's toy in his large fleshy hand.

He was a big man. It didn't worry me. The only thing that worried me, after seeing Toni's body and learning about Gail, was that when the time came I might accidentally break him or tear him apart. I kept reminding myself firmly that this was still a business matter and had nothing to do with love or hate.

"What's this?" he asked, holding out the little case he'd taken from my pocket.

"You've seen them before," I said.

"It's a drug case."

"If you know, why ask?"

"Why did you bring that and nothing else?"

He was puzzled. It was a good way for him to be. He thought I had some elaborate plan, and he wanted to know what it was before he disposed of me. If I'd told him I'd just come there cold to take him and his silly little gun barehanded, he wouldn't have believed me. So I told him.

"What do I need," I asked, "to take a loudmouth like you, Kroch? An armored regiment? But I had to bring something along to keep you quiet after I'd taken that popgun away from you and rammed it down your throat or elsewhere. It was either that or a rope, and I didn't have a rope."

His eyes narrowed dangerously; then he laughed. "You are bluffing, Eric. No, you are taunting me deliberately to make me angry. Why? What clever scheme have you got in mind?"

Off in the corner, Dr. Harold Mooney wiggled uncomfortably against his bonds and tried to say something through his gag. We paid him no attention.

"Clever?" I said to Kroch. "They wanted me to be clever, but I said what the hell it's just Karl Kroch, isn't it? If you want him, I'll go get him for you. Alive? Sure, I'll take him alive, I said. A dangerous man I might have to shoot, but not old Kroch."

His hand tightened on the gun—tightened and relaxed. He laughed harshly. "Childish, Eric," he said. "Very childish. But I wish I knew what you had in mind. "Then he frowned. "Why would your superiors want me alive? Why would they care?"

The truth was doing all right for me, so I stayed with it. "Well," I said, "they want to ask you some questions about a gentleman named Taussig, Emil Taussig. I said I was sure you'd be glad to cooperate after I'd worked you over a little."

He ignored the jab, still frowning. "Taussig?" he said. "The old man in Moscow? The white-haired old man who is so clever for the Communists? I only know what everyone in the business knows about Taussig. I have never even met him. Why would they want to question me about him, Eric?"

I laughed in his face. "Now who's bluffing, Karl? We have an odd notion you just might be working for that white-haired old man. As a kind of specialist, say. Not in Moscow, but right here."

He looked at me for a moment. He seemed displeased. He shook his head slowly. "But that is not so," he said, almost reproachfully. "You must know it is not so, Eric. You must know about me, by this time, enough. I gave you my name; you will have got a report by this time. You know who I am. You know where I came from. Why should you think such a thing of me?"

I had a sudden cold feeling that something was wrong, that everything was wrong. Gail had died before the case even started, as far as I was concerned; and now Kroch was being very sincere and earnest, and a little indignant, about something that shouldn't have bothered him a bit, if he was what we'd thought him. I remembered that I'd never been really satisfied with his behavior.

"What are you driving at, Karl?" I demanded.

"You do not understand?" he asked. He seemed surprised. "Why, I am Karl Kroch, *hein?* I might work for the Communists if I needed the money, that is true. What are politics to me? I am a professional, like you. But even a professional must draw the line somewhere, even in this decadent world we inhabit now with the Fuehrer gone. I am Karl Kroch. I do not work for Jews."

It was childish, if you wanted to look at it one way,

or vicious, if you wanted to look at it another. But it was also completely convincing. I didn't like to think what it implied.

I asked sharply, "Well, if you're not working for Taussig, damn it, why the hell are you trailing Olivia Mariassy around like Mary's little lamb?"

He stared at me. "But I was not following the lady scientist!" he protested. "Why would I do that? I was following you."

"*Me?*"

"I have been looking for you ever since last summer, Eric. Ever since I caught up with you in Redondo Beach a week ago, I have been following you, waiting for the right moment to deal with you properly."

And there it was. I didn't doubt him for a moment. There had been too many indications along the way; indications that I'd ignored or allowed myself to be talked into disregarding. I could have blamed Washington, I suppose, but I hadn't really put up a good fight for my doubts and reservations, not good enough to allow me to pass the buck now.

I'd sensed that Kroch was after me, of course. I'd been practically certain I was the one he'd been waiting for in Olivia's hotel room, for instance. But I'd assumed that I was merely an annoying detail he wanted to dispose of so he could get on with the main job. It had never occurred to me that I might be that job.

Yet as a man trailing Olivia, Kroch had never been completely convincing. As a man stalking me, whatever his motive, he became quite logical, if still a little melodramatic. I had to face the fact that I'd jumped to the wrong conclusion at the outset—we all had. Gail had died, Tom had died, and I might die, at the hands of the wrong man, a man who knew nothing significant about Emil Taussig. A lot of other people might also die...

"Did she not tell you?" Kroch said. "The beautiful lady in the Cadillac? I hoped she would live long enough to tell you about the ugly man who'd frightened her into the ditch. I wanted you to know I was after you, Eric."

"No," I said slowly. I remembered the policeman saying Gail had asked for me before she died. "No, she didn't tell me. She had no chance. She was dead when I got there."

"And the little girl here on the floor? Did she not tell you either? I told her to be sure to let you know Karl Kroch was after you and would strike when he was ready."

I said, "She said something like that, but I was working on another business and misunderstood your meaning."

"Misunderstandings," Kroch said sadly. "Always misunderstandings. I am sorry. I wanted to give you a fair chance, Eric. At least as much chance as you gave another man; a man we both remember."

I frowned at him. "What man?"

"A man named Von Sachs. General Heinrich Von Sachs. Now do you understand? Now do you remember?"

It was beginning to add up at last. "I remember Von Sachs," I said. "I don't remember you. You weren't down there in Mexico last summer when I went after him."

"No. I was in Europe on business for the General. I had been with him a long time, Eric; a very long time. I came back to find him dead and his great plan in ruins, due to one man. You, Eric."

"His great plan was a pipe dream," I said. "He'd never have made a fascist empire on this continent. I merely prevented an international mess by killing him."

"It is a matter of opinion," Kroch said. "But you did kill him. You played on his pride and his sense of honor; you taunted and insulted him until he consented to fight you with machetes, and then you cut him to pieces and killed him. He was a great man, but he had that weakness about honor, and you found it. When I learned what had happened, I swore I would find you and kill you the same way, Eric."

I said, "Any time. Bring on the machetes."

He laughed. "I am not so great a fool as that. What I mean is, you tricked and taunted my General into fighting under conditions favorable to you; now I have turned the technique against you, Eric. I did not think you were vulnerable through honor—it is not a common failing in the profession—but I did think you might be reached through your women. You Americans are very sentimental about women. And in spite of misunderstandings, it worked, did it not? You are here because of what I did to your women."

"Well, you might say that. What happens now?"

"What do you expect? I had hoped you would give me a better contest, but here we are. And now that you understand why you must die, I will kill you as you killed General Von Sachs. Slowly. Only, since I am not so good with edged weapons, I will not cut you to pieces, I will shoot you to pieces."

The gun in his hand steadied. I tried to remember the exact penetration of the little cartridge, in terms of one-inch pine boards—the usual standard—or human flesh. Well, one bullet had gone clean through Mooney's arm. It wasn't really a toy. I didn't think it would gain me anything to point out that I had not actually cut Von Sachs to pieces, I'd merely worn him down until I could drive my machete through his heart.

Taking aim, Kroch paused to glance at the gun in his hand. He chuckled, "It is a small-caliber weapon, Eric, shooting a very light cartridge. You will take a great many bullets before you die."

"I'm counting on that," I said.

He frowned quickly. I was ready when the pistol came steady again, and I knew I could make it. Now he wasn't even aiming for the chest or head; he wanted to have his fun before he killed me. You don't stop a man with that kind of peripheral marksmanship, not if you're shooting a .22. And as I'd told Olivia, while an angry man is usually easier to handle, he may be harder to stop. I had all the adrenalin I needed in my bloodstream to get me from here to there.

The little .22 settled on a point of aim and his finger put pressure on the trigger. I was aware of the strangled breathing of Harold Mooney, watching fearfully and making no effort to intervene. That was all right. I didn't want any help. I just wanted to get my hands on Karl Kroch. At that moment I was very happy he had no information anybody wanted. I didn't have to treat him gently. I didn't have to catch him and preserve him like a delicate scientific specimen. I could smash him like a cockroach, and I was looking forward to it; and I didn't care how big he was or how many guns he had. He was dead.

I was ready, but suddenly I became aware of a new sound: the sharp, hasty rapping of high heels in the corridor outside.

"Paul!" It was Olivia's voice, echoing throughout the hall. "Paul, where are you? Paul!"

Then she was in the doorway, and Kroch was distracted for an instant, and it was time to go and I went. He looked back to me. The little pistol started spitting as I threw myself forward. It sounded like a much larger weapon in the concrete room. Something nicked the side of my neck, something plucked at my shirt, something rapped at my thigh, and then all hell broke loose in that underground chamber.

It sounded as if the great coast guns that had once guarded this place had opened up, rapid-fire. Lead began bouncing from concrete to concrete in there. I saw Olivia in the doorway, following my instructions to the letter. Standing there in her good tunic dress and high heels, looking very lady-like and respectable, she was holding my sawed-off Smith and Wesson in both white-gloved hands and pulling the trigger smoothly and rapidly, wincing only a little at each crashing, reverberating discharge.

I started to shout at her. Hell, Kroch was mine. I tried to yell at her to leave him alone. I didn't want him full of bullet-holes, I wanted to kill him with my bare hands. Then common sense returned, a little, and I realized this was no place to be standing up in. I threw myself down, but a ricochet beat me to it. I felt a heavy blow above the ear, and things went bright red, and the redness faded slowly into black, but not before I'd heard the .38 click empty and Kroch fall.

20

"Paul," somebody said breathlessly. "Paul, wake up. Please wake up!"

I opened my eyes. Olivia was kneeling beside me.

"Kroch?" I whispered.

"He's dead. Paul, I'm sorry."

Well, she should be sorry, shooting down people other people had promised themselves the pleasure of killing... I pulled my thoughts together and realized she'd been apologizing for a different reason. She didn't know we'd been working on the wrong man. She thought she'd spoiled everything by putting Kroch where he'd never talk.

I remembered belatedly that I was an agent of sorts, not an avenging angel wielding the sword of retribution. There was a man I was supposed to find, a wicked old man with white hair. I wasn't any closer to finding him than I'd ever been. Or was I? I looked up at Olivia.

"What the hell are you doing here, anyway?" I asked.

"Well, you don't act very grateful!" she protested. When I didn't speak, she went on: "I couldn't let you get killed. It was suicidal, going after an armed, trained man with nothing but a hypodermic. It was crazy! I made Jack Braithwaite bring me here." She gave a strained little laugh. "I pointed your gun at him and made him drive me, just like in the movies. To hell with Emil Taussig! I don't give a damn if they never find him!"

"Don't swear, Doc," I said. After a little, I asked, "What's the damage?"

"You have a .22 bullet in your leg. It will have to come out later. I just stopped the bleeding temporarily."

I said, "Hell, we just dug a slug out of there last year. I seem to stop everything with that one damn leg. And my head."

"You may have a slight concussion." She held out her hand and showed me a flattened bullet. "That's what hit you. I didn't know they would splash and bounce like that. I thought I'd killed you!"

"Where's Jack Braithwaite?" I asked. I still didn't feel energetic enough to sit up and look around.

"Here, sir."

He came into my field of vision, and he wasn't alone. He was supporting the little blonde nurse on one arm. She was still in her uniform and her silly, formal hairdo; but she didn't look quite as fresh and glowing as she had in the Flamingo Lounge. She'd seen violence and death since then.

I said, "You seem to have misinterpreted my

instructions, Mr. Braithwaite. That's not the lady I instructed you to keep safe, if necessary at the cost of your life."

He licked his lips. "Sir, she had a gun—"

"So? Where did she shoot you? You don't seem to be bleeding very copiously. And what the hell are you doing here?" I asked Dottie Darden.

She looked indignant. "Why ask me? You sound as if I had a choice! When somebody has a little time, I'd appreciate being told what this is all about!" Anger made her strong enough to stand alone. She freed herself from Braithwaite's supporting arm. "Stop pawing me you... you phony Romeo! Using my apartment and pretending... Keep your hands to yourself!"

Olivia said to me, "I couldn't very well leave her by the telephone, Paul. I didn't think you'd want police interference. I made her come along."

I said, "I can't recall asking for any interference before twelve thirty-three." Her expression changed. I said wearily, "Ah hell. Pass that, Doc." She was still looking at me resentfully. I wasn't acting like a man whose life had been saved at the last desperate minute, I guess. Well, maybe I wouldn't have made it to Kroch after all. Nobody'd ever know now, and it wasn't worth arguing about. "And don't worry about our friend Kroch, he wasn't our man," I said. "Where's your tame Ben Casey, Doc? Where's the Apollo of the medical profession? I have a question to ask him as soon as he's recovered from his terrible ordeal, or maybe a little sooner."

"Harold?" She was still frowning, but in a different way. "What do you want to ask Harold?"

"I want to ask him," I said, "why he isn't dead." She was silent, and I went on. "I told you how it would be. I said Kroch would kill them both, and he should have. He killed Toni Vail."

"I know. I... I'm sorry, Paul."

I said, "What I want to know is, just what did Dr. Harold Mooney say that kept him alive? He must have talked very fast and he must have had some real good points to make. He must have been able to claim some friends in high places, for Kroch not to kill him, and I'm not talking about the Pensacola Chamber of Commerce or the American Medical Association. I want to know what he said. I want to know how a crumb like Mooney talked himself out of a bullet when Toni..." I checked myself. That was, after all, beside the point.

"Paul, please take it easy," Olivia said. "It isn't good for you to talk so much, or get so excited."

I laughed at that. I looked up at her and said, "We had it figured that Mooney was Kroch's accomplice at one point, remember? Well, we were wrong but we were only half wrong, as I see it now. He wasn't working for Kroch, but he was somebody's accomplice all right. And when it came to a showdown, with Kroch's gun pointing at his head, he used that somebody's name to save himself. He told Kroch something interesting enough so that instead of shooting him Kroch filed him for future reference, meaning to cash in on the information after taking care of me."

"Couldn't he—" Olivia hesitated. "Couldn't Harold just have offered money?"

"Is that what he says? Don't be naïve, Doc. You don't buy off people like Kroch, not with the kind of money Harold could offer. But sometimes you can arouse their curiosity by showing them a big game they might want to take a hand in, on one side or the other. It's the only deal Mooney could possibly have made, and he would have had to spill everything he knew, very plausibly, to make it stick. And if he could spill it to Kroch, he can spill it to me."

"No," Olivia said.

I couldn't read her expression. I looked quickly up at the other two standing over me, and they were regarding me oddly. They looked uneasy, maybe even guilty.

"What do you mean, no?" I asked sharply. "Where is he? You didn't let him get away?"

I tried to rise. Olivia held me down. She started to speak and changed her mind. There was a funny look about her eyes, as if she were close to crying. It was the blonde nurse who spoke at last.

"Dr. Mooney isn't… I mean, he's dead."

I stared up at her, and at Olivia, who turned away, biting her lip. I looked back to Dottie.

"The hell he's dead, Miss Darden! How come? He was thrashing around vigorously enough when I got here!"

She shook her head. "He was unconscious when we came in. Jack and I went right to him while Dr. Mariassy took care of you. Jack helped me cut him loose and get the gag off. He didn't respond. His pulse was very weak. I called Dr. Mariassy and we tried artificial respiration but it didn't help. We couldn't bring him around."

There was a little silence. I looked at Olivia. "I don't like asking, Doc, but it wasn't another of your ricochets?"

She shook her head. "No. There was no wound, Paul. He simply died. It may have been a heart condition, aggravated by fear and partial strangulation. The gag was very tight."

"Heart condition?" I said slowly. I heard myself laugh. It wasn't a very nice laugh. "Doc, you're kidding. Do you expect me to believe that the one man I needed to talk to died of heart failure? You're an optimist if you do." I looked at the other two. "Or somebody is!"

It was suddenly very quiet in the concrete room. They were all watching me. Olivia started to protest as I pushed myself up, but she thought better of it. She helped me rise. I had a sore leg, but it carried my weight after a fashion. I looked around. The place was getting pretty crowded, I decided. A couple more bodies, dead or alive, and we'd have to start turning away applicants.

Olivia said quietly, "I think you'd better say exactly what you mean, Paul. What are you hinting at?"

I studied her face for a moment. I looked at the other two. Olivia looked as if she was considering being angry. Braithwaite looked bewildered. Dottie looked scared. I didn't really blame her. It was quite a situation for an innocent young girl to find herself in, knee-deep in dead bodies—if she was an innocent young girl. At the moment

I would have put no trust in a white-robed angel from heaven complete with security clearance for Final Secret.

I limped over to the corner where Mooney lay. It wasn't really difficult. Getting down on my knees was the hard part. It had to be somewhere. I found it in the neck, at the edge of the hair.

"No wound, eh?" I said to Olivia, pointing to the tiny spot of blood.

She knelt beside me quickly, heedless of her nylons. Tending to the wounded had already given them enough of a beating on the concrete, I noticed, and another run wasn't going to make a great deal of difference. It was easier to look at her ruined stockings than to watch her pale face and wonder what was going on behind it.

She said, "Why… why, it looks like a hypodermic juncture!"

"Not really!" I murmured. "Doc, you astonish me!"

She looked at me. "Paul, what—"

"I gave you a message to give to young Braithwaite. In that message I said I might use the needle and a certain injection. Did you pass the word to Jack when you got in the apartment?"

"Yes," she said. "Yes, of course."

"Never mind that. The fact is that everybody here— everybody alive—knew there was a hypodermic available. Obviously somebody who's acquainted with the kind of kit we carry took advantage of that knowledge to silence Mooney in the confusion after all the shooting."

Olivia watched my face and didn't speak. Nobody

spoke. It was getting very tight in there, very close. I could feel something or somebody getting ready to break or make a break. Mooney had been killed to keep him from betraying one of three people. The person who'd done the job was waiting for me to put the finger on him—or her. I checked Mooney's clothes quickly. What I was looking for wasn't there. Toni was next. It wasn't nice, but I had to do it. She didn't have it either.

I struggled to my feet and limped over to Kroch where he lay face down in a pool of blood. He'd been thoroughly shot up and he'd done a messy job of dying. I felt in his coat pocket and my little drug case was still there. However, when I opened it, the hypo was missing as I'd expected. Having run the risk of picking the dead man's pocket for it, the murderer wouldn't be likely to run the risk of being caught returning it.

Something else was missing, too: half an ampoule, if that's the correct term, of the stuff we use when we don't want them to wake up. As I'd figured, under cover of the confusion, while the others were tending to the wounded and dying, the murderer had cleared my needle of the sleepy-stuff I'd been planning to use on Kroch and loaded up with a lethal dose of something permanent. Well, our techniques and equipment are fairly well known to the opposition, just as theirs are to us.

They were all watching me closely. I made a production of inspecting the case and Kroch's body. He didn't have it, either. That established the elements of the problem clearly: four concrete walls and a concrete floor, three people, one hypodermic syringe. I reached out and grabbed Kroch's fallen pistol out of the pool of blood. I aimed it at Braithwaite.

"You said you had a gun, Navy. I want it."

"But—"

"You have five seconds. At five, you're dead."

That was pure bluff, of course. I wasn't killing anybody. I'd lost one potential informant to death; I wasn't about to give away another.

Braithwaite swallowed. "Yes, sir." He reached gingerly into his pocket and brought out a revolver resembling the one I'd lent Olivia. I don't know what makes Washington so partial to the sawed-off little monsters, but they pass them around like chewing-gum samples.

"Lay it down and back away from it," I said. "You, Doc, on your feet. Get over there with him."

Olivia hesitated. Her eyes were wide and questioning, maybe hurt, but she didn't speak. After a moment, she rose and stood beside the boy. I looked at her bleakly. She could be very sweet and we'd had some fun, but I didn't know. I didn't know and I wasn't taking any chances.

"You've got a knife somewhere," I said. "I know because I gave it to you. It's no good for throwing, the balance is all wrong, so don't try. The gun I gave you, you shot empty. As for you, Miss Darden, stand right there with them. I don't know what you've got, weapon-wise, so don't scratch yourself anywhere, not even if it itches real bad."

I managed to get back to my feet. I switched hands

on the pistol, wiped my right hand on my pants, and switched back. I didn't really know whether Kroch's sticky little popgun would fire or not—it might even be empty—but neither did they. I gestured. They backed up. I moved forward and managed to get Braithwaite's weapon off the floor without falling on my face. A quick check told me it was fully loaded. I dropped the Spanish .22 into my coat pocket. I was in business as long as I could remain vertical.

Olivia said, "Paul, you're not doing your leg a bit of good. And you're acting like a madman. That blow on the head—"

"Let's postpone the diagnosis, ma'am," I said. "The treatment, too. I'm doing fine. I don't need medical attention. All I need is a hypodermic syringe. Just one little hypo, folks, and we can all go home."

"I don't understand," said Dottie Darden plaintively. "I don't understand—"

"You will," I said. "We might as well start with you. Take your clothes off."

It went over big. Olivia gasped and looked at me incredulously. Braithwaite stared at me with shocked indignation. The little blonde nurse thought I was pretty terrible, too.

"What?" she demanded.

"You heard me," I said. "And don't tell me I should pass you up because you're just an innocent bystander. You may be innocent, in one way if not another, but you're certainly no bystander. You worked for Dr. Mooney, you may or may not have slept with him—"

"I most certainly did not! Anybody who says so is a
dirty liar! And if you think I'm going to undress in front
of all these people—"

Olivia gave a sharp little laugh. "Don't be a hypocrite,
dear. You know you'll just love undressing in front of us;
you just wish we were all men!"

I said, "That'll be enough out of you, Doc." I looked
back to the blonde girl. "Come on, Dottie. Don't make
me get rough."

"Sir," Braithwaite said. "Sir, I don't think—"

"That's fine," I said nastily. "Let's keep it that way.
Dottie?"

She hesitated; then she gave a defiant little youthful
toss of the head that reminded me painfully of Antoinette
Vail alive—another kid who'd got mixed up in things
bigger than she was. Dottie threw an accusing glance at
Braithwaite, apparently blaming him for this humiliation
rather than me. She unbuttoned her uniform rapidly down
the front, slipped out of it like a coat, and passed it over.
A pink nylon slip came off over her head and followed the
uniform into my hand. There was nothing significant in
either garment. What remained wasn't worth taking off,
except perhaps the sturdy white nurse's shoes.

She started to unfasten her brassiere, more deliberately
now, even provocatively. She was beginning to enjoy
herself, I saw, in a wicked, perverse, abandoned way; she
was getting a charge out of standing there almost naked
with everybody watching her or trying not to watch.

The brassiere wasn't very substantial, and it obviously contained nothing but Dottie. I cleared my throat.

"That won't be necessary," I said. "Just take off your shoes and shake them out upside down… That's fine. I apologize, Miss Darden. When we get out of here, you can slap my face. Mr. Braithwaite, you're next."

He was quite red, and he was having a hard time keeping his eyes off the well-developed little girl beside him. Very calm and self-possessed, even smiling a little, she started putting her clothes back on as casually as if she were in her own apartment. You'd have thought no man was within miles of her as she dressed; certainly no young man with whom she'd been keeping company, to use the old-fashioned expression, earlier in the evening.

"Mr. Braithwaite," I repeated.

He started, "What, sir?"

"You, sir," I said.

Dottie giggled. "It's your turn, Jackie. Take them off, Lover-boy. Give us girls a thrill."

He glared at her, and at me. "Sir, you can't think I… You can't suspect *me*…!"

I said, "Sonny, you're temporary help. You haven't been trained. To the best of my knowledge, you haven't even been properly cleared yet. They just picked you off the street to help out in a minor way. Why did you want to leave a soft Navy berth to work for us, anyway? Sure, I suspect you. Somebody in this room slipped a hypo into Dr. Mooney. Why not you?"

I made a gesture with the gun. He undressed very

quickly. He was a good-looking young fellow, lean and sunburned. Dottie stared at him boldly and whistled admiringly to torment him. I wondered if he still thought her a nice kid. Well, her morals weren't my concern, and on the whole I found her attitude more convincing than if she'd put on a show of blushing embarrassment. After all, she was a trained nurse, and Queen Victoria was dead.

There was no hypodermic in Braithwaite's clothes. I threw them back to him and drew a long breath. We'd had a million laughs, and we'd seen a couple of fine young bodies, and we'd stalled long enough. I turned.

"Well, Doc," I said. "That puts it up to you."

Olivia faced me stiffly. She'd lost most of her unaccustomed lipstick during the course of the evening. She looked plain and rather dowdy, like the woman I'd met on the carrier a few days ago. She was back where she'd started. It was almost as if nothing had ever happened between us—almost but not quite.

There was the memory of that in her eyes. There was also the fact that, like me, she was somewhat older than the other two. I was asking her to discard her adult dignity, along with her clothes, in front of a couple of relative youngsters, one of whom she had reason to hate.

"I haven't got it, Paul," she said stiffly. "You're being absurd. Why should I kill Harold?"

Dottie laughed. "I can think of a reason!"

"Shut up," I said, and to Olivia: "Maybe Mooney wasn't killed to silence him. Maybe you just saw a chance for revenge and took it. You're a doctor, you know how to handle a needle, and maybe you can even tell the stuff that's deadly from the stuff that isn't, by smell or taste or something. Maybe the killing has nothing to do with what I'm after, but I've got to know who did it."

"Well, I didn't!" she breathed. "You've got to believe me—"

I said, "And maybe all this personal stuff between you and Mooney is sheer camouflage and there are things I don't know about. You hinted at something like that once, something very mysterious. Anyway, the hell with motives, for the time being. You told me definitely that Kroch was dead, Doc. That means you must have given him some kind of an examination. You were also called over to look at Mooney, says Miss Darden. From Kroch to Mooney, the way the needle went. Where is it?"

"I tell you," she said, "I haven't got it."

"I'm sorry. You're going to have to prove it just like the others did."

She said quietly, "I am not going to undress for you, Paul. You will have to… to strip me by force."

"I can do that, too," I said. "But why make it so tough if you've got nothing to hide? You're a doctor. Before that you were a medical student. What's so secret about the human body? I want that hypo, Doc. Or I want to *know* you haven't got it. Will it help if I say please?"

She shook her head minutely. She faced me, very straight, waiting. There was an odd kind of panic in her eyes, however; and I remembered that although I'd been allowed to make love to her, I'd never been allowed to see her naked: she'd kept a slip on or asked for a moment to change into a sexy nightie. Maybe she did have a thing about it, doctor or no. Maybe that was all it was. Or maybe she had something else to hide. There was only one way to find out.

I took a limping step forward. Olivia awaited me unmoving, but when I reached out to grasp the neck of her dress with both hands—one holding the gun—she drew a sharp breath and caught my wrists.

"No!" she gasped. "Paul, no! Please. I haven't got it. I swear. You can't—" she hesitated, and looked me in the eye, and said deliberately: "You can't do this to me, Paul!"

I returned the look. Hell, anybody can look. I said harshly, "You have to make this just as tough as you can, don't you?"

"Yes," she said fiercely, "yes, and when you've shamed me without finding what you're looking for, I hope you remember the rest of your life that I told you, swore to you, that it wasn't there!"

"I'll remember," I said. I shook her off and reached for her dress collar again. I saw defeat come into her face.

"Wait!" she gasped. "Wait, I'll do it." She hesitated. "Just let me… Just one thing first, Paul. A favor."

"Granted," I said. "With reservations. What is it?" She put out a hand. I stepped back quickly. "Hold it! What do you want?"

"Just the comb," she said.

"Comb?"

"The comb in your breast pocket. Just a cheap little

pocket comb. You can examine it carefully before you give it to me. I wouldn't want you to take any chances!" Her voice was bitter.

I regarded her for a moment, wondering what was in her mind. Then I shrugged, took the comb from my pocket, and gave it to her.

"Now what?"

"Now," Olivia said, and turned abruptly to look at Dottie Darden, "now I want permission to comb her hair."

There was a dead silence. Dottie raised her hands protectively toward the elaborate golden beehive—a little wispy now—that crowned her head, that any stupid policewoman would have made her take down as part of a thorough search. It wasn't the brightest evening of my life.

Olivia took a step forward with the comb, and Dottie broke for the door. I did have sense enough to stick my foot out and trip her. My wounded leg gave way, and I came down heavily beside her. I saw what she was doing, and grabbed for her to keep her from getting her hand to her mouth. It took a bit of brutal wrestling to get the death pill away from her.

Then I struggled to my feet and looked at the deadly little capsule in my hand and at the shapely little girl in hospital white, disheveled and dusty now, with her fancy hairdo disintegrating into sagging tufts and loops above a face that suddenly looked much older and not nearly as pretty as it had before.

Above one ear, like an exotic jewel, a bit of metal and glass gleamed among the tumbled blonde strands. She reached up, felt for it, found it, snatched it out, and hurled it at me. Her aim was poor. I heard it shatter against the concrete wall behind me.

"I'll never tell you anything!" she panted. "You can't make me talk!"

They always say that.

21

His name was Emil Taussig, but in St. Louis, Mo., he called himself William Kahn. He was an old man with white hair and kindly brown eyes. At least the people in the neighborhood were quoted later as saying they thought his eyes had looked kindly. I never got close enough, myself, to form an independent judgment. I was seventy-five yards behind him, across the street, and he was starting up the steps to his apartment house, when he fell down and died.

There was a doctor handy to make the examination and call it a coronary, carefully ignoring the tiny bullet-hole at the base of the skull. Karl Kroch wasn't the only one who could use a .22, and the caliber does have certain advantages. You can use an efficient silencer with it, for one thing. Silencers don't work too well with the heavier calibers.

After that a lot of things happened all over the country, as the shadowers that had been identified by other agencies were picked up in a nationwide net which had been prepared and held in readiness pending Taussig's demise. Many that had not been identified escaped, no doubt; and a few struck back. It didn't go quite as smoothly and bloodlessly as Washington had hoped, even with the top man dead, but when did it ever? There were also, I was told, a few international adjustments made at this time which may or may not have been connected with the affair.

That part of it didn't really concern me. Anyway, I was in the hospital with a badly infected leg. Another characteristic of the .22 is the fact that the greasy little bullet carries a lot of dirt into a wound; and maybe I hadn't stayed as quiet as I should. A gentleman from Washington visited me while I was still flat on my back and told me I was a hero and had probably saved the world or some small part of it. They've got a department for the purpose, I think. They call it internal public relations, or something.

I wanted to tell the guy to go to Florida and make his speech to a lady with a degree in astrophysics, but it wouldn't have been diplomatic. Neither did I succumb to the temptation to ask him just what the hell made him think any part of the world was saved. It was spring when I visited Pensacola again, on instructions from Mac.

"The lady wants you to sign some papers," he'd said, in Washington. "I told her you'd stop by when you could."

"Sure."

"Incidentally, you may run into young Braithwaite down there. He didn't work out for us. He's back with his ship." Mac threw me a glance across the desk. "You gave him a rather rugged introduction to the work, Eric. There was no need for him to witness the interrogation of the girl, for instance."

"He'd had a part in catching her," I said. "I thought he might as well get used to seeing a job through."

"After watching the I-team at work on Miss Darden—she died afterward, you know—Lieutenant Braithwaite apparently decided he didn't want any part of the glamorous life of an undercover agent." Mac was looking at me in a speculative way. "Perhaps that was what you had in mind, Eric?"

"Perhaps," I said. "Is my, er, wife still living at the same address?"

She was, Mac said, but when I wanted to call the house from the Pensacola Airport, I couldn't find the name Mariassy in the phone book. Then I realized what I was doing wrong and turned to another section and there it was: Corcoran, Paul, 137 Spruce, 332-1093. It gave me a funny feeling to see the name again. I hadn't used it since the previous autumn.

I called the number and got a maid who said Miz Corcoran was out but if I was Mr. Corcoran I was supposed to pick her up at the lab—Building 1000 at the Naval Air Station. She was expecting me.

A taxi took me through the gate and across the big base, past a drill field where some kind of a military ceremony was in progress. There was a reviewing stand that seemed to contain a lot of naval rank. Solid masses of lesser officers stood on the side lines. The colors were just coming onto the field, followed by a long column of naval aviation cadets or midshipmen or whatever the Navy calls them.

My driver managed to find a street that wasn't blocked and got me down to the waterfront, from where I could look out across the harbor at Santa Rosa Island, but I couldn't see anything that looked like a deserted fortification out there. I probably wouldn't recognize it in daylight, anyway. I could still hear the brassy sound of the Navy band as I went to the front door of the building. That was as far as I got, not having the particular clearance required to penetrate farther into the sacred mysteries of science.

"Mr. Corcoran?" said the elderly guard. "Yes, sir. Please have a seat. I'll call Dr. Corcoran. She's expecting you."

Then she was coming down the stairs. At least the approaching woman looked in a general way like the woman I remembered from last fall, but her hair was styled in a different and softer way, and the lipstick was obviously firmly established now, smoothly and expertly applied. She was wearing a brown sweater and a tailored brown skirt that made her look tall and slim. Only the legs hadn't changed. They were still very fine, nicely displayed by nylons and high heels.

I got to my feet, not knowing exactly what to expect. She came across the lobby and put her arms around my neck and kissed me hard, which surprised me in more ways than one. We hadn't parted exactly friends.

I heard her voice in my ear. "Play up, damn you! The guard's a terrible old blabbermouth. Don't just stand there!" Presently she stepped back and said a little breathlessly, "I've missed you, darling."

"I tried to get back sooner, but they've been keeping me busy. You're looking great, Olivia."

"Am I?" She did something embarrassed and feminine with her hair. I remembered that she'd always been a great girl for fussing with her hair after a kiss. "Did you have a nice trip?" she asked.

"Moderate. It was a little rough over the mountains, but not too bad."

"I'm sorry I couldn't meet you at the airport but something came up. The car's right outside." She took my arm and led me out into the sunlight. "Thanks, Paul," she said in a different tone. "Some of them in there have been acting as if they didn't really believe I had a husband. The guard will put them straight, the old gossip." She laughed apologetically. "After all, I do have a career and a reputation to maintain, now that I'm no longer a desperate undercover agent."

"Sure."

"Do you want to look around? I can't show you our work, of course, but they've got some interesting equipment here that isn't too highly classified, like the human centrifuge and the rotating room in which they study problems of equilibrium... Well, it was just a suggestion Paul?"

"Yes?"

"I wanted to apologize afterward, but you were gone."

"Apologize? What for?"

"For making it harder for you. That night. There was a reason why I just *couldn't* undress in front of everybody. I didn't mean all the nasty things I said." She hesitated and glanced at me with a hint of mischief in her eyes. "Would you really have stripped me naked?"

"Sure," I said.

She laughed softly. "I'm glad. I don't like people who talk tough and act mushy. I don't like people who mix sentiment with business or science. At least you're a consistent monster. I am glad to see you again, Paul. I mean, really."

"I like you, too, Doc," I said. "Shall we go sign those papers?" I mean, it was nice talking over old times, but somebody had to bring the meeting to order.

She stopped smiling. "Yes," she said. "Yes, of course." She still had the same little black Renault; she hadn't even managed to put many miles on it, I noticed. I remembered to fasten my seatbelt without being told. She drove, but after a couple of blocks we were turned back by a base policeman: the ceremony was still going on. The next street wasn't any better. We were at the side of the field but they wouldn't let us drive along it. I heard commands being snapped out. The cadets, or whatever they were, were about to pass in review.

"Come on," I said. "Leave it here and let's look. I'm a sucker for parades."

She looked unenthusiastic, but I pulled her out of the

car and dragged her over to the field and found a spot where we could get up close. They were coming along the edge of the field toward us, four abreast, in perfect step, with the colors out front. I remembered to take off my hat. The military spectators were saluting.

Olivia nudged me, and I looked where she was looking, and there was Lt. (jg) Braithwaite among the others near the reviewing stand, in uniform, holding his salute smartly as the flag passed. He looked happy and untroubled. He was back where he belonged.

The cadets marched by, looking sternly ahead, and the band followed, belting out "The Stars and Stripes Forever." It was all very corny and obsolete, of course. There had been a time when they would march right up to the guns like that, with the drums going, but we don't fight that way any more. Perhaps it's just as well. Maybe we're better off just leaving the drums out of it.

The Navy musicians were right on top of us now, giving Sousa everything they had. I knew Olivia wanted to stick her fingers in her ears, but I was remembering standing on the island of an aircraft carrier bathed in a different kind of sound, watching the jets being catapulted into the wind.

I remembered that I'd been feeling rather superior to the kid pilots and their noisy toys that day last fall; but now I came to the conclusion that I hadn't had a very sound basis for that feeling. They might not be much good at doing what I did, but then, there were times when I wasn't very good at it myself. And I'd play hell trying to do what they might have to do some day, Braithwaite included. It was a humbling thought.

"Let's blow," I said, and ten minutes later we were entering the house with the picture window, in the development with the French-curve streets. It wasn't entirely a good feeling, coming into the familiar room after the better part of a year. "Well," I said, "show me where to make with the pen and paper, Doc. Where's this stuff you want signed?"

"There isn't any stuff," she said. "That is, the lawyers have something, I think, but it isn't here."

I turned to look at her. There wasn't anything to say, so I didn't say it. I waited.

"I had to get you down here," she said.

"So you could lure me to the laboratory and show me off as your husband?"

"Yes," she said. "That was one thing. Don't say anything, Paul. There's something I want you to see before you say anything. This way." She walked quickly across the living room and down the hall past the door of the big bedroom I remembered. She opened a door on the other side of the hall. "In there," she said, stepping back to let me by.

I moved past her and stopped. It was a small room. The wallpaper had bunnies on it. There was a crib, and in the crib was a baby, an unmistakable human child. It was sound asleep, wearing blue knitted booties. As a onetime daddy, I knew that blue booties meant a boy.

I turned to look at Olivia. Her face was expressionless.

She put a finger to her lips. I went back into the living room, leaving her to close the door. When I heard her coming, I was standing by the picture window, thinking that I would never understand why people built picture windows just so they could look across a street at other people's picture windows; but that was kind of beside the point.

"Now do you understand?" she said, beside me. "I told you it wasn't my secret. It was his. He had to have a name. Well, he has one. It's the name of a man who doesn't really exist, but that doesn't matter. It's legal, and that's what counts. Nobody can take it away from him."

I turned to look at her. She looked slender and attractive in her nicely fitting sweater-and-skirt outfit. I remembered the loose, clumsy clothes she'd worn. All the pieces fitted into the puzzle perfectly.

"I was going to be very clever," she said quietly. "I'd agreed to marry an unknown government man—very reluctantly, of course. And I planned to arrange it so that you... so that the government man, after the wedding, would never protest that the child wasn't his. He might guess, but he'd never know. But of course you do know whose it is."

"Now that you say it."

"When I learned I was pregnant, I went to Harold and, well, you know what happened that day. I probably didn't make much sense to you where Harold was concerned. I despised him and still... and still, I'd loved him once, and I was carrying his child." She drew a long breath.

"Well, he's dead. He'd never have married me, anyway. The most he would have condescended to do was operate. You know what I mean. I'm not really the maternal type, but I didn't want that."

I looked at her. "Just what do you want, Olivia?" I asked.

She faced me steadily. "His name is Paul Corcoran, Junior. I suppose he'll grow up being called Junior. Anyway, he has a name. There was a little pause. I'd like him to have a father, too," she said. "Not much of a father, necessarily. Just a man who comes around now and then, a man who's off on business most of the time, but seems to be a pretty nice guy when he does turn up."

"I'm not a pretty nice guy," I said.

She smiled. "I know that, and you know it, but he doesn't have to."

I said, "You're working hard for this kid."

She hesitated. "It isn't entirely for the kid, Paul or Matt or whatever your real name is. I… it's been a very lonely winter."

There was another little pause. "Sure," I said. "But you're a good-looking woman. You can find somebody who can make it a full-time job."

"I'd hate him," she said. "I'd hate him, going to his stupid insurance business or law office with his stupid briefcase every day of the year. I'd despise him. I'd be brighter than he, and I'd have to hide it."

"You're brighter than I am," I said.

"Technically speaking, maybe, but it doesn't matter,"

she said. "With us, it doesn't matter. Don't make me throw myself at your head, Paul. We're the same kind of people, in a funny sort of way. We could make it work. It's as much marriage as either of us needs, but we both need that much. You, too."

I said, "You're a cold, calculating wench, Doc."

She shook her head minutely. "No," she said softly. "No, I may be calculating but I'm not… not cold. You know that, unless you've forgotten."

I said, "I haven't forgotten."

We stood by the big window, facing each other warily, almost like enemies. Then I had her in my arms, slim and hard and responsive; and then I was looking over her shoulder at something lying on the little table behind her.

"What is it?" Olivia whispered after a moment. "What is it, darling? What's the matter?"

I let her go and walked past her. I picked up the knife and remembered who had given it to me. I remembered how Gail had died, and why. I remembered kneeling by Toni's body, knowing that I was responsible for her death, too, because anybody with whom a man in my line of work associates is bound to attract danger sooner or later.

Olivia was watching me. Her face was pale. "I put it out so I wouldn't forget," she said. "I thought you'd want it back. The knife, I mean. Paul, what's the matter?"

I didn't know how to say it without sounding like a pompous jackass or a self-pitying martyr to duty, or something. I didn't know how to tell her that she was a swell girl and I liked her proposition fine but she'd better find herself a man who wasn't a human lightning rod, if not for her own sake then for the baby's. I was glad when the telephone began to ring noisily. Somehow I knew it was for me. With that kind of timing it could only be Mac. It was.

"Eric? I was hoping to catch you before you left," he said. "Have you finished your business with the lady? Can you get over to New Orleans fast? You know the number to call when you get there."

I looked at Olivia. "Yes, sir," I said into the phone. "I'm finished here. I'll be there before midnight."

I stuck the knife in my pocket, picked up my hat, and left. The first three steps toward the door were the hardest. After that it got easier, a little.

ABOUT THE AUTHOR

Donald Hamilton was the creator of secret agent Matt Helm, star of 27 novels that have sold more than 20 million copies worldwide.

Born in Sweden, he emigrated to the United States and studied at the University of Chicago. During the Second World War he served in the United States Naval Reserve, and in 1941 he married Kathleen Stick, with whom he had four children.

The first Matt Helm book, *Death of a Citizen*, was published in 1960 to great acclaim, and four of the subsequent novels were made into motion pictures. Hamilton was also the author of several outstanding stand-alone thrillers and westerns, including two novels adapted for the big screen as *The Big Country* and *The Violent Men*.

Donald Hamilton died in 2006.

COMING SOON FROM TITAN BOOKS

The Matt Helm Series
BY DONALD HAMILTON

The long-awaited return of the United States'
toughest special agent.

Death of a Citizen
The Wrecking Crew
The Removers
The Silencers
Murderers' Row
The Ambushers
The Ravagers (February 2014)

COMING SOON FROM TITAN BOOKS

PRAISE FOR DONALD HAMILTON

"Donald Hamilton has brought to the spy novel
the authentic hard realism of Dashiell Hammett;
and his stories are as compelling, and probably
as close to the sordid truth of espionage,
as any now being told."
Anthony Boucher, *The New York Times*

"This series by Donald Hamilton is the top-ranking
American secret agent fare, with its intelligent
protagonist and an author who consistently writes
in high style. Good writing, slick plotting and
stimulating characters, all tartly flavored with wit."
Book Week

"Matt Helm is as credible a man of violence as has
ever figured in the fiction of intrigue."
The New York Sunday Times

"Fast, tightly written, brutal, and very good…"
Milwaukee Journal